CARRYING THE
SHEIKH'S BABY

CARRYING THE SHEIKH'S BABY

HEIDI RICE

MILLS & BOON

First published in Great Britain 2018
by Mills & Boon, an imprint of HarperCollins*Publishers*
1 London Bridge Street, London, SE1 9GF

Large Print edition 2019

© 2018 Heidi Rice

ISBN: 978-0-263-08231-9

MIX
Paper from
responsible sources
FSC
www.fsc.org   FSC™ C007454

This book is produced from independently certified
FSC™ paper to ensure responsible forest management. For
more information visit www.harpercollins.co.uk/green.

Printed and bound in Great Britain
by CPI Group (UK) Ltd, Croydon, CR0 4YY

To my best mate Catri O'Kane,
who helped me brainstorm this story
on a road trip in West Texas!

CHAPTER ONE

Dr Smith, you need to come to my office ASAP. You have a very important visitor who cannot be kept waiting.

CATHERINE SMITH PEDALLED through the gates of Cambridge's Devereaux College at breakneck speed, her boss Professor Archibald Walmsley's curt text making sweat trickle down her forehead and into her eyes.

Braking at the side of the redbrick Victorian monolith that housed the faculty offices, she leapt off the bike and rammed it into the cycle rack before swiping her brow. Rounding the building, she spotted a limousine with blacked-out windows and diplomatic flags parked in the no-parking zone by the front entrance. Her heart-beat kicked up several extra notches.

She recognised those flags.

So that solved the mystery of who had come to visit her: it had to be someone from the Narabian embassy in London. Panic and excitement tightened around her ribs like boa constrictors as she raced up the steps—her mind racing ahead of her.

A visit from the Narabian embassy could either be very good, or very bad.

Walmsley—who had taken over as Devereaux College's dean after her father's death—was going to kill her for going over his head and applying for official accreditation for her research into the recent history of the secretive, oil-rich desert state. But if she got it, even he wouldn't be able to stand in her way. She'd finally be able to get more funding for her research. Her heart thudded against her chest wall in a one-two punch. She might even get permission to travel to the country.

Surely this had to be good news. The country's ruler, Tariq Ali Nawari Khan, had died two months ago after a long illness and his son, Zane Ali Nawari Khan, had taken over the throne. A darling of the gossip columns as a baby—Zane Khan was half-American, the product of Tariq's short-lived marriage to tragic Hollywood starlet Zelda Mayhew—he'd disappeared from the public eye, especially after his father had won custody of him in his teens. But there had been several credible stories the new Sheikh was planning to open the country up, and bring Narabia onto the world stage.

Which was why she'd made her application—because she was hoping the new regime would consider lifting the veil of secrecy. But what if she'd made a major mistake? What if this visit was actually very bad news? What if the diplomat was here to complain about her application? Walmsley could use it as an excuse to end her tenure.

She rushed down the corridor towards Walmsley's office, breathing in the comforting scent of lemon polish and old wood.

The pulse of grief hit her hard as she took the stairs to her father's old office. This place had been her whole life ever since she was a little girl, and her father had taken over as the new dean. But Henry Smith had been dead for two years now. And Walmsley had wanted her gone—as a reminder of the man whose shadow he'd lived in for fifteen years—for almost that long.

Buck up, Cat. It's time. You can't spend the rest of your life hidden behind these four walls.

Turning the corner to Walmsley's office, she spotted two large men dressed in dark suits standing guard outside his door. Her heart rammed into her throat, the crows of doubt swooping into her stomach like dive-bombers.

Why had the Narabian embassy sent a security detail? Wasn't it a little over the top? Maybe Walmsley's reaction wasn't the only thing she had to worry about?

She brushed her hair back from her face and retied the wayward curls to buy time. The snap of the elastic band was like a gunshot in the quiet hallway. Both men stared at her as if she were a felon, instead of a twenty-four-year-old female professor with a double PhD in Middle Eastern studies. They looked ready to tackle her to the ground if she so much as sneezed.

She forced herself to breathe. *In, out—that's the spirit.*

'Excuse me,' she murmured. 'My name's Dr Catherine Smith. Professor Walmsley is expecting me.'

One of the man mountains gave a brusque nod, then leaned round to shove open the door. 'She is arrived,' he announced in heavily accented English.

Cat entered the office, the hairs on her neck prickling alarmingly as Walmsley's head snapped up.

'Dr Smith, at last, where have you been?' Walmsley said, his exasperated enquiry high-pitched and tense.

Cat jumped as the door slammed shut behind her. Her anxiety levels increased, the boa constrictors writhing in her belly. Why was the dean fidgeting like that with the papers on his desk? He looked nervous, and she'd never seen him nervous before.

'I'm sorry, Professor,' she said, trying to read her boss's expression—but his face was cast into shadow by the pale wintry light coming through the sash window behind him. 'I was in the library. I didn't get your text until five minutes ago.'

'We have an esteemed visitor, who is here to see you,' he said. 'You really shouldn't have kept him waiting.'

Walmsley held out his arm and Cat swung round. The prickle of awareness went haywire. A man sat in the leather armchair at the back of Walmsley's office.

His face was cast into shadow. But even seated he looked intimidatingly large, his shoulders impressively broad in an expertly tailored suit. He had his left leg crossed over his opposite knee, one tanned hand clasping his ankle. The expensive gold watch on his wrist glinted in the sunlight. The pose was indolent and assured and oddly predatory.

He unfolded his legs and leaned out of the shadows, and Cat's wayward pulse skyrocketed into the stratosphere.

The few photographs she'd seen of Sheikh Zane Ali Nawari Khan didn't do him justice. High slashing cheekbones, a blade-like nose and his ruthlessly cropped hair were offset by a pair of brutally blue eyes, the colour of his irises the same true turquoise his mother had once been famous for.

He had clearly inherited all the best genes from both sides of his bloodline—his features a stunning combination of his father's striking Arabic bone structure and his mother's almost ethereal Caucasian beauty. In truth, his features would almost be too perfect, but for the scar on his chin—and a bump in the bridge of his nose, which marred the perfect symmetry.

Cat's lungs contracted.

'Hello, Dr Smith,' he said in a deep cultured voice, his English still tinged with the lazy cadence of America's West Coast. He unfolded his long frame from the chair and walked towards her—and she had the weirdest sensation of being stalked, like a gazelle who'd accidentally wandered into the lion enclosure at London Zoo. She struggled to get her breathing back under control before she passed out at his Gucci-clad feet.

'My name is Zane Khan,' he said, stopping only a smidgen outside her personal space.

'I know who you are, Your Highness,' she said breathlessly, far too aware of her height disadvantage.

He spoke again in that same clipped, urbane tone. 'I don't use the title outside Narabia.'

Blood rushed to her face and flooded past her eardrums. Then a dimple appeared in his left cheek, and her lungs seized again.

Oh, for Pete's sake, a dimple? Isn't he devastating enough already?

'I'm sorry, Your High… I mean, Zane.' Heat charged to her hairline when his lips quirked.

Oh. My. God. Cat. You did not just call the ruler of Narabia by his first name.

'Sorry. I'm so sorry. I meant to say Mr Khan.'

She sucked in a fortifying breath and the refreshing scent of citrus soap, overlaid with the spicy hint of a clean cedarwood cologne, filled her nostrils. She shuffled back, and her bottom hit Walmsley's desk.

He hadn't moved any closer, but still she could feel that concentrated gaze on every inch of her exposed skin.

'Are you here about my request for accreditation?' she asked, feeling impossibly foolish.

Why on earth would he have come all this way, to see her, over something that could be sorted out by one of his minions in the Narabian embassy in London?

'No, Dr Smith,' he said. 'I'm here to offer you a job.'

Zane had to resist the unprecedented urge to laugh when Catherine Smith's hazel eyes widened to the size of dinner plates.

She hadn't expected that. Then again, he hadn't expected her. The only reason he'd come in person was because he already had a business meeting in Cambridge today with a tech firm who would be helping to bring superfast internet access to Narabia. And because he'd been furious once he'd received the reports from his tech people that someone at Devereaux College had been doing research on Narabia without his express permission.

He hadn't bothered to read the file they'd

emailed to him about the female academic who had asked for accreditation. He'd simply assumed she would be frumpy and middle-aged.

The very last thing he'd expected was to be introduced to someone who couldn't be much older than a high-school student, with eyes the colour of caramel candy. She looked like a tomboy, dressed in slim-fit jeans, a pair of biker boots and a shapeless sweater that nearly reached her knees. Her wild chestnut hair—barely contained by an elastic band—added to the impression of young, unconventional beauty. But it was her candy-coloured eyes that had really snagged his attention. Wide and slightly slanted, giving them a sleepy, just-out-of-bed quality, her eyes were striking, not least because they were so expressive, every one of her emotions clearly visible.

'A job doing what?' she said, her directness surprising him as she eased further back against her boss's desk.

Looking past her, he directed his gaze at Walmsley. 'Leave us,' he said.

The middle-aged academic nodded and shuffled out of the room, well aware his department's funding was at stake because of this woman's research.

The woman's eyes widened even more, and he could see the jump in her pulse rate above the neckline of her bulky sweater.

'I require someone to write a detailed account of my country's people, the history of its culture and customs to complete the process of introducing Narabia on the world stage. I understand you have considerable knowledge of the region?'

His PR people had suggested the hagiography. It was all part of the process of finally bringing Narabia out of the shadows and into the light. A process he'd embarked upon five years ago when his father had let go of his iron grip on the throne. It had taken Tariq Khan five years to die from the stroke that had left him a shadow of his former self, during which time Zane had managed to drag the country's oil industry out of the dark ages, begin a series of infrastructure projects that would eventually bring electricity, water mains and even internet access to the country's remote landscape. But there was still a very long way to go. And the last thing he needed was for any gossip to get out about his parents' relationship and the difficult nature of his relationship with the man who had sired him. Because that would become the whole story.

He shrugged, the phantom pain searing his shoulder blades.

This woman's work threatened to throw the book he had planned to commission—stressing the country's adaptability and new modern outlook—into stark relief if she found out the sordid truth about how he had come to live in Narabia. But shutting her down wasn't the right response. He had always been a firm believer in challenging problems head-on. 'Never trust anyone' had been one of his father's favourite maxims—and one of the many harsh lessons Zane had learned to embrace wholeheartedly.

'You want me to write a book on the kingdom?' She seemed astonished. He wondered why.

'Yes, it would mean accompanying me to Narabia. You would have three months to complete the project but I understand you've already spent over a year doing research on the kingdom?' Research he needed to ensure hadn't already uncovered information he wished to conceal.

She moistened her lips, and his gaze was drawn to her mouth. Even though she appeared to wear no lipstick, he became momentarily fixated by the plump bow at the top, glistening in the half-light. The surge of lust was surprising. The women he slept with were usually a great deal more sophisticated than this woman.

'I'm sorry. I… I can't accept.'

He dragged his gaze away from her month, annoyed he'd become fixated on it. And annoyed more by her response to his proposal. 'I assure you the fee is a lucrative one,' he said.

'I don't doubt that,' she said, although he suspected she had no idea how lucrative the fee he would propose actually was, certainly more than an academic could make in a decade, let alone three months. 'But I couldn't possibly write a comprehensive account in that time. I've only done preliminary research so far. And I've never written something of that magnitude. Are you sure you don't want a journalist instead?'

No way was he inviting a journalist to pry into his past. That sort of uncontrolled intrusion into his affairs was precisely what this carefully vetted account was supposed to avoid.

Heat pulsed in his groin at her surprising show of defiance. He ruthlessly ignored it. However much he might want to devour that cupid's bow mouth, he was not in the habit of seducing subordinates—especially not ones who looked about eighteen years old.

'How old are you, Dr Smith?' he asked, abruptly changing the subject.

She stiffened and he suspected he'd insulted her with the question. She must be used to people questioning her credentials, which was hardly surprising—she didn't look old enough to be in college, let alone to hold two PhDs.

'I'm twenty-four.'

He nodded, relieved. She was young and probably sheltered if she'd managed to gain that much education so quickly, but not that young.

'Then you are still at the start of your career. This is an opportunity for you to make a name for yourself outside the—' his gaze drifted over the worn leather textbooks, the musty academic tomes, all dead history to his way of thinking '—world of academia. You wanted official accreditation for your research into Narabia...' Accreditation he would give her once he had final say on the content of her work. 'This is the only way you will get it.'

He waited for her to absorb the offer, and the threat—that if she didn't agree to his proposition, any chance of getting official accreditation would be lost.

It didn't take long for the full import of his position to sink in—her expressive face flushing with something akin to alarm.

'I could continue my work without the accreditation,' she said, but her teeth pulled at her bottom lip. The nervous tug sent another annoying jolt to his crotch, but also revealed her statement for what it was—a heroic bluff.

'You could. But your tenure here would be withdrawn,' he said, his patience at an end. No matter how attractive or heroic she was, he did not have time to play with her any longer. 'And I would personally ensure you were not allowed access to any of the materials you need to continue researching my country.'

Her eyebrows shot up her forehead. The flush on her cheeks highlighted the sprinkle of freckles across her nose. 'Are you... Are you threatening me, Mr Khan?'

Placing his hands into the pockets of his suit trousers, he stepped closer. 'On the contrary, I'm offering you a chance to validate your work. Narabia is a fascinating and beautiful place—

which is about to come out of its chrysalis. And finally fulfil its potential.'

That was the end game here: to turn the country into somewhere that could embrace its cultural heritage without being held back by it.

'How can you write about a country you've never seen? A culture you've never experienced? And a people you've never met?'

The passion in Zane Khan's eyes only made the cerulean blue more stormy and intense. And deeply unsettling.

He's calling you a coward.

The implication stung, touching a nerve she had spent years cauterising. But really, how could she dispute his assessment?

Ever since she'd arrived in Cambridge, arrived at Devereaux College, she'd immersed herself in learning because it made her feel safe and secure.

But ever since her father's death, she'd wanted to spread her wings, to stop being scared of the wanderlust she'd banked so carefully as a child.

Don't be so boring, darling. Daddy won't know if you don't tell him. What are you? A cat or a mouse?

The image of her mother's bright—too bright—smile and her milk-chocolate eyes, full of reckless passion, flickered at the edge of Cat's consciousness like a guilty secret.

Don't go there. This has nothing to do with her. This is all about you.

She forced herself to meet Zane Khan's pure blue eyes again, dark with secrets her research so far had only hinted at. This man was dangerous to her peace of mind, but why should that have anything to do with her professional integrity? So what if she felt completely overwhelmed and she'd only been in his presence for five minutes? Surely that was just a by-product of all the things that had held her back for so long. Confidence had to be earned. And that meant facing your fears. And not being a coward.

All you have to do is believe you can, Cat. Then you will.

Her father's supportive voice and the encouragement he'd given her when she'd been crippled with anxiety on her first day of primary school, of secondary school, of sixth-form college, of university and then graduate school, echoed through her head.

A bubble of excitement burst in her blood. Yes,

the thought of this trip was terrifying. But it was way past time she stopped living in her comfort zone. She was twenty-four years old. And she'd never even had a proper boyfriend—the flush rode up her neck—which probably explained why she'd practically passed out when she'd met Zane Khan.

She'd pored over pictures and artefacts from Narabia, been captivated by the country's stunningly diverse geography and its rich cultural heritage—but she'd only been able to scratch the surface of its secrets. She already knew she needed to experience the country and the culture first-hand to validate her work. The chance to experience what might well be a tumultuous time in the country's history was also tantalising—professionally speaking.

And the only time she would have to spend in Zane Khan's company would be for her research.

'Would I be able to have full access to the archives?'

'Of course,' he answered without hesitation.

An anthropological book detailing the country's rich cultural heritage, its monarchy and the challenges they were facing made sense. Zane

Khan and his own past were surely at the centre of that.

'I'd also like to interview you at some point,' she said before she could chicken out.

She saw the flicker of something brittle and defensive in his eyes and the muscle in his jaw tensed. 'Why would that be necessary?'

'Well, you're the country's ruler,' she said, not sure why she was having to explain herself. 'And also because you had a Westernised childhood—you would have a unique perspective that spans both cultures.'

'I'm sure I can arrange to speak to you at some point,' he said, but his tone was strangely tight. 'So do we have a deal?'

She let out a deep breath, feeling as if she were about to jump off a cliff—because in a lot of ways she was… But she'd been waiting for an opportunity like this for a long time.

You don't want to be a mouse for ever.

'Okay—you've got a deal,' she said, the surge of excitement at her own daring almost overwhelming her panic.

She reached out her hand, but then long strong fingers folded over hers—and she yearned to snatch it back. His grip was firm, impersonal, but the rush of sensation that raced up her arm was anything but.

'How long will it take you to pack?' he asked.

'Umm… I should be able to fly over in a week or so,' she said, grateful when he released her hand. She needed to rearrange her teaching schedule, pack up her flat on campus and give herself more time to make absolutely sure she was happy jumping off this cliff.

'Not good enough,' he said.

'I beg your pardon?' she said, disturbed by the no-nonsense tone, and the sensation still streaking up her arm.

'I'll have the contract drawn up and delivered to you within the hour. Is five hundred thousand pounds sufficient for your input on the project?'

Half a million pounds!

'I… That's very generous.'

'Excellent, then we will leave for Narabia tonight.'

We…? Tonight…? What…?

'I…'

He held up his hand, and the feeble protest got stuck in her throat.

'No *buts*. We made a deal.' He took a phone out of his trouser pocket, and walked past her.

The two bodyguards and Walmsley, who must have been lurking outside the door, all snapped to attention as he opened it.

So Zane Khan didn't just have that disturbing effect on her.

'Dr Smith will be leaving on my private jet tonight,' he announced.

Walmsley's mouth dropped open comically, but Cat didn't feel much like laughing.

Zane glanced over his shoulder. 'A car will arrive in four hours to take you to the airport,' he said.

'But that's not enough time,' she managed, past the constriction in her throat. What exactly had she just agreed to? Because she was starting to feel like a mouse again. A very timid, overwhelmed mouse, in the presence of a large, extremely predatory lion.

'Anything you need will be provided for you,' he said, cutting off any more protests by lifting the phone back to his ear and striding away down the corridor, with the two bodyguards flanking him.

Cat watched his tall figure disappear round the corner, her breath locked in her lungs and her stomach free-falling off the cliff without the rest of her.

Problem was, she hadn't had the chance to jump off this particular cliff—because she'd just been pushed.

CHAPTER TWO

C AT ARRIVED AT the private airfield outside Cambridge four and a half hours later, still dazed from her meeting with the Narabian ruler.

Is this actually happening?

The arc lights from the airfield hangar illuminated a sleek private jet painted in the gold and green colours of the desert kingdom's flag.

The driver, who had arrived on the dot of eight o'clock at her flat on campus, hauled her borrowed rucksack out of the back of the limousine and escorted Cat across the airfield to the plane's steps.

A man appeared at the aircraft's door, dressed in a robe and a traditional Narabian headdress. He lifted the battered bag off the chauffeur's shoulder and ushered her onto the plane, introducing himself as Abdallah, one of the Sheikh's personal servants.

She was led through the cabin—the plush leather seats and polished teak tables offset by thick wool carpeting—into a private bedroom at the end of the plane.

'You will be served dinner in here once we are airborne,' the man said in perfect English, putting her bag onto one of the cabin's armchairs. She stifled the sting of embarrassment at the sight of the hastily packed rucksack marring the butter-soft leather upholstery. 'Suitable clothing has been made available for your stay in Narabia,' Abdallah announced, his gaze flicking discreetly over her attire—and making her acutely aware of the battered boots, jeans and second-hand sweater she hadn't had a chance to change out of. There was no censure in his tone, but still she felt impossibly awkward and ill-prepared. Especially when the servant slid open the door of a built-in wardrobe to reveal an array of dark flowing robes.

'His Excellency, His Divine Majesty, has asked that you dress appropriately when leaving the plane—and limit your questions to myself or the other palace staff at all times.'

Cat nodded mutely, her nervousness accompanied by a tingle of irritation. It seemed His Divine Majesty was used to giving orders and having them obeyed without question. But how was she going to be able to do the research she needed to do on Narabia's customs and culture if she was not able to be a free agent?

'Is Mr Khan on the plane?' she asked.

The man's eyebrows rose a fraction before he spoke. 'His Excellency, His Divine Majesty, the Sheikh of Narabia is *flying* the plane, Dr Smith. He has asked me to assist you in any way you desire.'

The tightness around her ribcage eased at the thought she wouldn't have to see Zane Khan again until they landed. But then she felt disappointed in herself.

This was going to be an adventure. An adventure she would one day be able to tell her grandchildren. Events had moved much faster than she was comfortable with. But was that really a bad thing?

Impulsiveness was a trait she'd quashed throughout her childhood and teenage years—and she'd persuaded herself it was a good thing she hadn't had the chance to quash it this time.

Unfortunately, that didn't make what lay ahead of her any less intimidating or overwhelming. And Zane Khan's presence did make it that much harder to process, because she didn't seem to be able to breathe properly when he was near her—let alone process her thoughts. But his decision to start dictating her every move before they'd even left the UK did not bode well for her work.

She wanted to do a thorough job. Which meant she would have to get up the guts to confront His Divine Majesty if she had to.

'We will be landing in Narabia at eight tomorrow morning,' Abdallah informed her, his implacable gaze revealing nothing. 'His Excellency, His Divine Majesty, will speak with you then, before we proceed to the Sheikh's palace.'

Cat's pulse hammered her collarbone. The Sheikh's palace had been built over five hundred years ago on a natural spring, and its architectural splendour was rumoured to rival that of the Taj Mahal, but no photographs existed of it. Only a few pencil drawings done by a British explorer in the nineteen twenties.

She would be the first outsider to see it in generations. She took a deep breath and let it out again to contain the leap of excitement.

Strike one for impulsiveness.

'Thank you, I look forward to seeing it,' she said, barely able to stifle her grin as Abdallah excused himself and left.

Her breathing clogged again though, as the plane's engines rumbled to life. She strapped herself into the leather passenger seat and imagined Zane Khan's long fingers handling the controls. Her stomach lifted into her throat as the plane raced down the tarmac and rose into the night sky above Cambridge.

There was a three-hour time difference between the UK and Narabia, which gave her approximately nine hours to figure out how she was going to handle her interaction with His Divine Majesty the next time she saw him.

She counted her breaths in and out, as the lights of Cambridge disappeared under the cover of clouds.

Not hyperventilating would be an excellent start.

After a three-course dinner—consisting of Narabian delicacies in a tantalising combination of African and Middle Eastern flavours—Cat managed a fitful four hours' sleep on the luxurious bed. The last time she woke, to the efficient purr of the plane's engines, the desert landscape was visible through the cabin windows, only a few thousand feet below.

With only an hour till they landed she rushed her shower—while struggling to get her head around the idea of having a shower on a plane—then dug out her meagre supply of make-up. She rarely wore it, but in this instance the smudge of eyeshadow and the slick of lip gloss should help boost her confidence and her courage.

Donning one of the robes proved a great deal more challenging. The flowing floor-length garment was made of gossamer-thin black silk with stunning gold embroidery at the cuffs and hem. The fitted bodice hooked up the front right to the neck, and included a matching scarf. But what exactly was she supposed to wear underneath it? Was the robe supposed to be worn as a dress or an overgarment?

Even in spring, the desert kingdom would be extremely hot. But the only other items in the closet were other similar robes and an array of delicate underwear. Heat incinerated her cheeks as she ran her fingertips over the transparent lace.

Just the thought of wearing the skimpy undergarments with only a thin layer of silk to cover them in front of Zane Khan had her hyperventilating again. She was nervous enough already.

Of course, he wouldn't be able to see she was virtually naked beneath her robe, but she would know.

In the end, she settled for putting on her sturdy cotton bra and panties and one of her maxi summer dresses under the robe. Made for summer in Cambridge, not spring in Narabia, the dress was a great deal heavier than the lightweight material of the robe, and it made the robe itself a bit snug, but the added layer helped to slow her rampaging pulse. After wrestling with the hooks to fasten the front of the robe over her breasts, she tied back her damp hair with an elastic band, draped the exquisitely embroidered scarf over her head and tied the ends at the back of her neck.

Strapping herself in for the landing, she devoured the dramatic sight of the rocky terrain as the plane skimmed over a mountainous region to touch down at a deserted airfield. But as the plane taxied and then came to a stop in front of a large, sleekly modern glass-and-steel hangar, her stomach didn't quite land with it.

When Abdallah arrived ten minutes later, she'd repaired her make-up twice—and debated about fifty times whether to simply step out of the cabin. Perhaps they had forgotten she was on the plane?

'His Divine Majesty awaits your presence,' Abdallah announced, picking up her rucksack.

Play it cool, and remember to keep breathing.

She smoothed sweaty palms down the robe, feeling the bulk of fabric where her dress tightened the fit.

As she stepped out of the cabin her gaze locked on a group of men dressed in robes standing beside the plane's open door. Or one man in particular, who stood head and shoulders above the rest.

As if he had sensed her presence, Zane Khan turned to face her, and her breath locked in her lungs again.

Breathe, Cat, breathe.

She struggled to regulate her lung function before she passed out. She'd never seen anything so magnificent—or so masculine—as the Sheikh of Narabia in his traditional ceremonial garb.

Her gaze stole up his frame, taking in every aspect of the striking outfit.

Knee-high leather boots shone in the blazing desert sunlight stealing in through the cabin's door, and moulded to impressive calf muscles.

Black cotton trousers hung loose around his long legs to give him ease of movement but did nothing to disguise the powerful muscles in his thighs. A silk sash that matched the extraordinary blue of his eyes provided a startling splash of colour around his lean waist. The long flowing cloak he wore trailed to his knees but any semblance of modesty was belied by the black tunic that hung open at his neck in a deep V, revealing tantalising wisps of chest hair. But it was his dramatic headdress—draped to shade his head and shoulders and the back of his neck and held on with a jewelled gold band around his forehead—and the sabres glinting on his hips and attached by across-the-shoulder leather straps that had Cat's breath gushing out.

No wonder they call him the Divine Majesty.

He didn't only look magnificent, he looked indomitable—a man entirely at one with his heritage and his own masculinity. Those pure blue eyes seemed to bore into her through the silk of her own robe—right through the fabric of her dress and the sturdy cotton of her underwear to her palpitating heart. She thanked God she had decided to wear the extra layers, because even with them on she felt naked—every inch of her skin tingling with awareness.

'Dr Smith,' he said in that rough, commanding baritone. He held out a hand and hooked a finger, directing her to come to him. 'I see you found the clothing,' he said.

All her senses screamed in unison—although she wasn't sure what they were screaming for her to do, fall into his arms, or run like hell in the opposite direction, because both options seemed viable.

You're a cat, not a mouse. Move.

Breathing deeply, she stepped forward and laid trembling fingers in his wide palm. He folded her arm into the crook of his elbow and she found herself drawn forward and tucked against his side.

'Let's get to the car before the plane becomes an oven,' he said, the conversational tone doing nothing to calm her rampant heartbeat.

She bobbed her head, feeling like a compliant puppet.

They descended the plane steps together. The desert heat was immense, even so early in the morning, the sun creating mirages on the tarmac and a heat haze on the horizon. But she burned hottest where their bodies touched, the gossamer silk of her robe and the thick cotton of her dress feeling heavier than armour and yet offering her no protection whatsoever from the subtle shift of muscle and sinew where his forearm tensed against her side.

Sweat pooled in her collarbone and trickled down her temple, her heart beating so fast and so loudly she wondered if he could hear it, because it sounded like a machine gun to her.

They walked through a phalanx of servants and bodyguards, all of whom dropped to one knee as Zane passed, the look of awe on their faces something she was very much afraid had been reflected on her face when she'd first walked out of her cabin.

She tried to school her features. Just because Zane Khan was treated like a living god in Narabia, he was still only a man.

As if in acknowledgement of this fact, Zane stopped to speak to several of his subjects as he passed, introducing her to two men in particular as the heads of his ruling council. Four SUVs were parked in a line at the end of the welcoming committee, their paintwork gleaming in the sunshine and looking strangely incongruous given the ancient power being honoured by all present. A guard rushed forward to whisk open the back door of the car in the middle, which looked as if it was half limousine, half all-terrain vehicle. The flags, bearing the insignia of the ruling house of Nawari, marked it out as the Sheikh's vehicle. Stepping to one side and finally letting go of her, Zane swept his arm forward, directing her into the interior.

She bent to climb inside, but was only halfway into the car when she came to an abrupt halt. Her knees slammed onto the seat tangled in the robe, her palms slapping on the cool leather, her bottom jutting up in the air as she struggled to free herself. She flapped her feet furiously, as embarrassment scorched her insides, but all she managed to do was lose her sandals. She was stuck fast, hideously mindful of Zane standing behind her, being presented with her upraised bottom.

A husky chuckle made her humiliation complete before strong fingers snagged her ankle, sending sensation skimming up her leg and weakening her already straining knees.

'Hold still,' said the deep voice, now rough with amusement. 'The hem is caught.'

Seconds later, the forward momentum had

her landing on the seat with a loud 'oomph' in a sprawl of silk, cotton, bare legs and bruised pride.

She scrambled to right herself, her cheeks now hotter than the Narabian sun despite the cool interior of the air-conditioned car. Deep chuckles reverberated off the leather interior as Zane folded himself into the seat beside her and the door slammed behind them. The car drove off.

'Neatly done, Dr Smith,' he said, obviously enjoying himself immensely at her expense.

But then she looked into his face. He seemed so much younger, almost boyish, his usually severe expression softened by laughter, his shoulders vibrating so hard, the sabres were jingling like bells.

A bubble of laughter burst out. She covered her mouth, but as he continued to chuckle, she couldn't seem to stop herself from joining him. Suddenly they were laughing together, his husky guffaws matched by her higher-pitched giggles. For a few precious moments, the nerves and anxiety in her stomach dissolved and she felt like a child, free and unencumbered by the sizzling sexual tension that had characterised all her interactions with Zane Khan so far.

'I can't believe I made such a monumental tit of myself,' she finally managed as the laughter slowed to a few intermittent chuckles.

'Neither can I,' he said, huffing out one more laugh.

He wiped his eyes with the corner of his robe. And a burst of euphoria rose up her torso. She had no idea why, but she had the strangest feeling Zane Khan didn't laugh nearly often enough. Dignity and pride seemed a small price to pay for managing to demolish the austere facade— even if only for a few moments.

'Here.' He leaned towards her and she saw her sandals resting in his large palm. 'You dropped these.'

'Oh, thank you.' They shared a few more errant chuckles as she plucked them out of his hand.

But as she absorbed the warmth of his touch that lingered on the soft leather, the last of her laughter trailed away, and a heavy sense of intimacy descended.

She could feel his gaze as she fumbled with the hem of her robe and her dress before slipping the footwear back on. She rearranged her skirts to cover her legs, unbearably aware of him once more.

'I think I see what the problem is,' he murmured.

'The problem?' she asked, making the mistake
of glancing at him.

All traces of the boyish amusement were gone
as his gaze roamed over her clothing.

'The robes are designed to be worn with as little beneath them as possible.' Was it her imagination or had his voice dropped several octaves?
'Adding extra layers makes them more cumber-
some and tends to inhibit the cooling effect.'

'O-oh, I see,' she stuttered.

The hot brick in her stomach plunged between
her thighs and her nipples tightened as they made
the rest of the drive through the desert in silence.

Ruining the cooling effect completely.

What the hell? I have an undiscovered toe fetish.
Zane absorbed the rocky, forbidding landscape
as the car crested the rise and headed into the
desert valley towards the Sheikh's palace, far
too aware of the woman sitting stiffly in the
seat beside him—and the burn on his fingertips
where his hand had connected with her ankle.
The sight of her unpainted toes and bare feet as
she'd slipped on her sandals hadn't helped con-

tain the surge of lust that had been tormenting him ever since she'd stepped out of her cabin.

His imagination had gone into overdrive as soon as she'd appeared, everything the ankle-length robe with its intricate beading disguised somehow even more erotic than her tomboy jeans and shapeless sweater of the day before.

He shifted in his seat as the palace came into view. He heard her sharp intake of breath. The enormous five-hundred-year-old structure with its domed turrets, lavish mosaic tiling, walled gardens and courtyards and intricately carved arched walkways was a truly magnificent example of Moorish architecture that would awe any new visitor. He had been awestruck himself sixteen years ago when he'd seen it for the first time as a confused teenager, using belligerence to hide his fear—only to discover that misery, not magic, lurked behind the golden walls.

He dispelled the unpleasant memories as the car approached the town of Zahari—which had sprawled around the walls of the palace for over three hundred years—and sailed through the marketplace. Traders and customers stood at a respectful distance, many of them bowing their heads or dropping to their knees as the car passed.

'Is that customary? For your subjects to kneel before you?' Catherine Smith's soft voice yanked him back to the present and tugged at his groin in a way he had been trying to ignore ever since they'd left the plane.

He would have to get his reaction to this woman under control. It could only be a result of the sexual drought he'd suffered in recent years, ever since his father's illness and death had required him to spend so much time in Narabia.

'It is not required,' he said, aware of the sharp tone when she flinched.

It wasn't her fault she had an unpredictable effect on him and his sex-starved libido. Any more than it was her fault the delicate arch of her instep and those slim, straight toes had him obsessing about sucking and licking each one in turn, then slowly inching the layers of clothing up her slim curves to discover exactly what treasures lay between her toned thighs.

He shook his head, and attempted to focus on the haze that shimmered on the palace's golden walls as the car drove through the gates and entered the forecourt.

Seducing Catherine Smith would be a foolish move, which could easily backfire. He had no intention of giving her more access to him than was strictly necessary. She'd already requested an interview, something he'd had to force himself not to refuse out of hand. And he did not like the way she'd looked at him a moment ago, as if she somehow knew it was a long time since he'd had cause to laugh so spontaneously. Part of her job here was to study the behaviour and customs of Narabia's people, but he did not intend to let her study him.

The thought of the indulgent burst of laughter and what it might have revealed dampened the heat in his groin as the car drove through the grove of palm trees, around the fountain that adorned the entrance to the palace and glided to a stop by the steps leading up to the arched entrance to the main residence. Climbing out of the vehicle, he offered a hand to Catherine.

One glimpse of those damn toes though, and the blood surged right back into his pants.

She exited the vehicle with a great deal more grace than she had used getting into it. But the memory of her pert bottom outlined in silk failed to alleviate the heat swelling in his groin.

The silk covering her hair did nothing to disguise the riot of chestnut curls. He clenched his fists to quell the urge to plunge his fingers into the unruly locks. Having this woman in the palace for three long months was going to be more of an ordeal than he'd thought when he had offered her the commission.

She tilted her head to view the building. 'It's even more breathtaking than I expected.'

The breathy comment was artlessly erotic, skimming over his skin. The heavy weight of the sabres jostled his hip as he stood aside to let her precede him up the steps.

'Your Excellency, welcome home,' his majordomo greeted him. As efficient and imperturbable as always, Ravi didn't even flick an eyelash at the sight of his companion, or the evidence that Zane had arrived back from a business meeting in the UK with an unknown female guest. Clapping his hands, Ravi barked out a series of orders in Narabi at the line of servants, who rushed forward to collect the luggage.

'This is Dr Smith,' Zane said. 'She is an academic scholar and is going to be writing a book about Narabia's customs and its cultural history. She will be staying in the women's quarters.'

As far away from my toe fetish as possible.

'Yes, Your Excellency,' Ravi said before turning to Catherine and bowing. 'Welcome to Narabia, Dr Smith.' He held out his arm. 'If you come this way, I will escort you to your quarters.'

'I'll escort her to the women's quarters myself,' Zane cut in.

Both Catherine and Ravi looked at him, obviously startled by the offer. He was a little startled himself—etiquette for someone of her station certainly did not require him to give her a personal escort.

But he found he couldn't regret the impulsive decision as he led her through the palace towards the separate walled estate in the grounds where the female staff and his unattached female relatives lived and he watched her reaction.

Ever since he had arrived in Narabia, the palace had felt like a prison to him. The ornate splendour both oppressive and confining, the grandeur only emphasising the unhappy history contained within these walls.

But as the scent of lemons and limes refreshed the air around them, and he watched the vivid colour on Catherine's cheeks intensify and her caramel gaze sparkle with fascination, her head swivelling back and forth as she took in the sights before her, for the first time in his life, he could see past the darkness too.

He pushed the romantic thought aside, determined not to read too much into the buoyant feeling at Catherine's exhilarated response.

She was the first foreign visitor to see this place since his mother. Of course she would be awestruck. The Sheikh's palace was a beautiful and elaborate prison, but a prison nonetheless, something his mother had found out to her cost.

Just because Catherine in her naivety couldn't see that, it didn't mean it wasn't true.

After all, it was his job to keep her from discovering that truth.

Walking through the Sheikh's palace was like stepping into an alternative world—as exotic and mesmerising and exciting as Narnia behind the wardrobe. As Cat absorbed the myriad sights and sounds and scents, she struggled to ignore the man beside her, whose stern demeanour was at odds with the cascade of emotions making her heart hammer like a timpani drum.

Unlike the rest of the palace, which had been calm and quiet and steeped in an austere reverential solemnity, the women's quarters were a hive of chatter and activity—until the women spotted the Sheikh in their midst.

A few of them tugged veils over their faces as Zane passed, but many of the younger ones did not, some even chatting behind their hands before they bowed or curtsied. Zane seemed impervious to the attention, but it was clear to Cat she wasn't the only woman aware of the magnificent figure he cut.

The sunlight dazzled her, leaving her dazed when they stepped out of the searing heat of the forecourt into a walled garden. Shaded by trees laden with all manner of exotic fruit and an array of lush plants, the garden was laid out along a series of mosaic pathways punctuated by fountains and other decorative follies. More women, many of them wearing brightly coloured silk robes, sat on intricately carved marble benches, but sprang to their feet to curtsy as she and Zane passed.

They turned a corner and Cat's mouth fell open. A stunning pool, its blue-green water fed by a man-made waterfall, stretched out before them, creating a cooling centrepiece to the lavish garden. On the outside, the quarters had seemed austere, but this garden was like a secret paradise.

Zane proceeded to lead her through a citrus grove that skirted the pool. The refreshing scent of oranges and lemons filled the hot, dry air. They walked down another path shaded by towering palm trees, the raised flower beds on either side filled with a profusion of showy blooms and manicured shrubs.

Finally they left the garden and entered a cool domed courtyard, this one covered with a painted ceiling. Like the rest of the palace, the chamber was intricately and elaborately decorated, with stunning marble and mosaic tiling. Lounging areas filled with cushions and draped with exquisitely embroidered silk hangings made the space feel welcoming rather than forbidding. The warm air was cooled by huge ceiling fans, which covered the sound of laughter and talking coming from the interior of the building with the swish of the blades.

Large arched doorways led off the central chamber. Each smaller chamber contained a disparate group of women indulging in different pursuits. One group was seated in a circle on the floor sewing a tapestry, another group was cooking in a kitchen equipped with state-of-the-art stainless-steel surfaces—the aromatic scents of frying spices making Cat's tummy grumble—and yet another chamber appeared to be a classroom, where one woman was scribbling maths problems on a whiteboard for the others. It occurred to Cat that the juxtaposition of female learning, new appliances and traditional crafts was like a microcosm of how the new Sheikh's modernising influence was affecting Narabia's ancient society. But as before, all conversation ceased as they walked past, only making Cat more aware of how revered Zane was by his people. And the centuries-old power that emanated from him.

She wondered why he had offered to take her to her quarters. Because she felt both hideously exposed while also being invisible.

Stop hiding, darling. And say hello to Mummy's friend.

The jolt of memory made her steps falter. Zane's arm tensed as she stopped.

'Are you okay?' he said. His voice sounded rough, and she realised it was the first time he'd spoken to her since they had left the palace forecourt.

'Yes, yes, I'm fine. I'm just a little tired. And overawed.'

Or rather a *lot* tired and overawed. Why else would she start thinking about her mother?

And reading far too much into a simple courtesy. Obviously, Zane Khan had only offered to escort her to her quarters to be polite. And now she was making a massive meal of it.

He searched her face in a way that only made her feel more uncomfortable, then clicked his fingers above his head. 'Who here speaks English?' he asked, addressing a group of young women who had gathered to watch them from a respectable distance.

A teenage girl stepped forward, covering the bottom of her face with her veil, her dark eyes alive with curiosity.

'What is your name?' he asked the girl.

'Kasia, Your Divine Majesty,' she answered in faltering English.

'This is Dr Catherine Smith. You will serve her for the duration of her stay here at double your normal salary. Make sure she has everything she desires and she does not go anywhere unescorted. Do you understand?'

The girl nodded furiously, her cheeks flushed

as she dropped to one knee. She didn't reply, clearly speechless at being addressed directly by the Sheikh. But Cat felt the prickle of dismay at his instructions. Why did she have to be escorted everywhere?

'Kasia will show you to your quarters,' he said, addressing Cat, that searing, all-seeing gaze silencing the unruly thought. 'She will accompany you wherever you go. It is very easy to get lost in this place.'

The prickle of dismay was crushed by panic.

Exactly how powerful was this man? Could he read her thoughts?

As Kasia, her new minder, led Cat up a flight of stairs to a mezzanine level, she stole one last glance over her shoulder.

Zane Khan strode back through the gardens towards the entrance to the women's quarters. His powerful figure cut a dark swathe through the colourful clothing of the women and the garden's exotic flora.

The soft edges she had glimpsed in the car had been sheared off, as if they had never existed. As soon as they had arrived at the palace, he had become every inch His Divine Majesty again, entitled to rule over everyone he surveyed... Including her.

Her rapid heartbeat sank into her abdomen. But it couldn't disguise the pang of regret at the thought that the man she'd glimpsed in the car had never been more than a figment of her over-active—and far too romantic—imagination.

CHAPTER THREE

OVER THE FOLLOWING fortnight Cat buried herself in the project, which helped ground her and dispel any more of the foolish feelings about Zane that had assailed her on her arrival.

The first job she set herself was to become more fluent in the spoken language, so she didn't feel like such an interloper. Although Kasia had overstated her command of English, she was smart and eager to help Cat integrate into the society of women in the palace. As they tested out their faltering language skills on each other, Kasia soon became a friend, and also an invaluable research assistant, proving a font of knowledge when it came to documenting Narabia's customs.

Kasia and the other women who Cat had interviewed though, were less informed on the subject of the Nawari royal family. And Zane in particular. No one seemed to know anything about when he had first come to the palace, or more specifically his relationship with the former Sheikh. Either that or they had been told not to say anything.

Cat convinced herself she was being paranoid. Why would Zane have hired her to do a job like this if he had something to hide? Especially as he had arranged for her to go on a series of 'fact-finding missions'.

But even though Cat had found the day trips—to a host of local businesses, architectural wonders and even to one of his council meetings—informative and interesting at first, after two weeks of these carefully orchestrated excursions, her initial suspicions had begun to return.

She was learning how to converse in Narabi with Kasia's help, but she was never allowed to speak to anyone not specifically sanctioned to speak to her by the Sheikh. The bodyguards and advisors who accompanied her wherever she went seemed to be under strict instructions about whom to allow her to speak to. And nothing she said or did could influence them to loosen their hold on her schedule.

Zane meanwhile had been unavailable since that first night. And the interview he'd promised her had yet to materialise.

At first Cat had been grateful for his absence, aware of how overwhelming she found his presence. But as the days passed, and her conversations with Kasia and the other people in the palace brought up questions she wanted to ask that only Zane could answer, her gratitude began to turn to frustration—with herself as much as him.

She wanted this project to be a seminal study of a country and a people whose lives and culture had been almost entirely cut off from the outside world for generations. But for that she needed proper access to all walks of Narabian society, and more access to their Sheikh, especially as he appeared to be the driving force behind all the changes taking place.

Her academic integrity was at stake. Not only that, but Zane had promised her the interview when she'd agreed to take the job.

She could keep her strange reaction to him in check. She wasn't used to male attention, and certainly not the attention of a man who exuded enough testosterone to arouse a stone. But she couldn't let her social ineptitude screw up this project. And she only had three months to write this study, so she couldn't waste any more time pandering to her own insecurities.

But two weeks after arriving in Narabia, she didn't seem to be any closer to getting the promised interview with its Sheikh. Ravi had been unfailingly polite and helpful, but whenever she'd asked about Zane, she'd been fobbed off with a series of vague excuses.

His Excellency was too busy. His Excellency was out of the country. His Excellency didn't have the time to deal with the project today.

So yesterday, she'd decided to write the Sheikh a note—reminding Zane of his promise to grant her an interview.

One curt line scrawled in black ink on a piece of cream notepaper was the result.

Ravi will arrange an interview at my convenience, when I have the time.
ZK

'The Sheikh, he writes to you like a lover.'
Cat glanced up to find Kasia grinning at her.
Cat blushed as she scrunched the note up in her fist and tossed it in the waste bin by the writing desk she had been given. 'He writes to me like a tyrant, more like.'

'What is this *tyrant*?' Kasia asked, testing her increasingly fluent English.

Cat searched for the word in Narabi. But of course there wasn't one, because *tyrant* was an insult, and apparently being an obstructive jerk was perfectly okay if you were the Sheikh in this country. 'Someone who never lets you do what you want to do,' she said.

The girl grinned. 'What is it you wish to do?'

'I need to speak to people outside these walls,' she said in her own faltering Narabi. 'I want to interview a much bigger cross section of Narabian society.'

She'd like to interview Zane Khan too, but she figured that was way outside Kasia's remit.

'Why do you not go to the marketplace? There are many people of Narabia there.'

'I would, but I can't go anywhere unaccompanied,' she huffed, the frustration starting to choke her. 'And all the visits we've been on so far, I haven't been allowed to talk to anyone properly.'

'You could come with me to buy the herbs and spices for eating tomorrow.'

Cat's heart hammered against her ribs. Why

had she assumed that Kasia never left the palace? 'That's… Thank you. That's a brilliant idea.'

The thought of finally taking her research to the next level had her pulse pounding in her ears. She should have had the guts to do this a lot sooner. After all, Zane hadn't specifically said she couldn't leave the palace. It wasn't Zane holding her back, it was her own conformity. And cowardice.

'Your Excellency, there is news from the women's quarters.'

Zane glanced up from the letter he was writing to find his major-domo standing at the arched entrance to his private office. Ravi's face was drawn, and his hands clutched together.

Terrific, what the heck has Catherine Smith done now?

The woman was proving much more troublesome that he had anticipated.

No way was he arranging an interview with her before he was sure he could control the emotions that had fazed him when she had first arrived. But she'd proved surprisingly persistent and demanding, making repeated requests to see him even though he'd made it quite clear he was not available.

'What is it, Ravi?' he snapped, putting his pen down. 'Please tell me this isn't another request for an interview from Dr Smith,' he said. 'Because the answer is still no.' And he'd already told his major-domo he did not want to be bothered with her requests from now on—because all that did was trigger more of the desires he was currently trying very hard to suppress.

'No, Your Excellency.' Ravi's usually implacable expression became tight with concern. 'I have just been informed Dr Smith is no longer in the palace.'

'What?' The punch of anxiety hit Zane square in the solar plexus. 'Then where the hell is she?'

'We do not know, but we believe she may have left to go to the spice market with her servant, Kasia.'

Zane jerked out of his chair, his heart starting to kick his ribs like his thoroughbred Arabian stallion, Pegasus.

'How long have they been gone?' he demanded as he charged across the room.

'No one has seen them for several hours.'

Several hours.

His thundering heart crashed into his throat.

Anything could have happened in that time. Catherine was a stranger here—how well did she even speak the language? He should never have left her to her own devices. The panic tightened around his heart, reminding him of being a boy in LA and waking up in the middle of the night to find himself alone in his mother's apartment. A gaping hole opened in the pit of his stomach, the very same one that had appeared every time he'd had to scramble out of bed and track down his mother in one of the neighbourhood bars.

Not the same thing, damn it.

Zelda had been fragile, mentally and physically, and a chronic alcoholic. Catherine Smith was none of those things.

But still the gaping hole refused to disappear as he marched down the walkway towards the palace's stables.

He had to get her back before she got hurt, or worse.

'Why wasn't I told about this sooner?' Zane demanded, channelling the old fear into anger at his major-domo.

'I am sorry, Your Divine Majesty,' Ravi panted, breathing heavily as he raced to keep up with Zane.

'Get me a robe and have Pegasus saddled,' he shouted at one of the stable boys as he arrived in the equine palace, the comforting scent of hay and manure doing nothing to stem the fear gripping his insides.

'Your Excellency? There is no need for you to venture o-out...' Ravi stammered. 'I have the palace guard ready to search the marketplace on your orders.'

'I'll lead the search party,' he said.

Ravi returned with his robe. Zane shrugged it on, then took the *keffiyeh*. Securing the traditional headscarf with an *agal* rope, he covered his mouth and nose. It was almost noon, so it would be a hot dusty ride in searing heat. But he'd be damned if he'd let the palace guard conduct the search without him.

Pegasus arrived, stamping his hooves, his nostrils flaring as he shook his head against the bridle. Taking the reins from the stable boy, Zane grabbed the pommel on the horse's saddle, stuck his boot into the stirrup and leapt onto the highly strung stallion as the horse charged out of the yard.

The hooves of the guards' horses clattered behind him as the palace gates were rolled open.

The sun blinded him as Pegasus flew out of the grounds, and past the palace's walls. The horse took the unpaved road down towards Zahari. People scattered, many dropping to their knees as they recognised him and his guards.

As they approached the labyrinth of streets leading to the old town and the women's spice market, the colourful silks on the clothing stalls waving like flags, anger rose up to cover the gaping hole.

When he found Catherine, she was going to feel the full force of his fury, for defying his orders. And putting herself in unnecessary danger.

If he found her.

'She says Tariq was a cruel Sheikh.' Kasia relayed the information in English as Cat nodded, scribbling on the notepad she'd brought with her.

They had been at the market for over two hours, she'd taken photos of the amazing sights and sounds, had absorbed the workings of the place and revelled in the chance to finally see a side of Narabian society without close supervision. But speaking to Nazarin, an elderly stallholder, was the first opportunity she'd had to talk to anyone specifically about Tariq Ali Nawari Khan's forty-year reign.

Nazarin's hands were gnarled and stained from years spent dying cloth to sell at the market. Her accent had been far too thick for Cat to decipher, but with Kasia's translation help she had been a font of knowledge about the Nawari family thanks to her experiences going to the palace to deliver cloth.

'She says he was very cruel to his son,' Kasia added.

Cat's head jerked up from her notes. 'Are you talking about Zane?' she said in Narabi to Nazarin.

The woman stared for a moment, obviously taken aback by the informal address. Then she nodded and rushed off a torrent of words, but the guttural inflections were impossible for Cat to understand.

She had to wait patiently for Kasia to finish listening to the woman's words. Eventually her friend turned to Cat, her eyes round with shock. 'She says, yes, the new Sheikh. The one from

America. When the boy came to the palace, she says he tried many times to escape and he was punished harshly for this disobedience.'

'Punished? How?' Cat whispered, shocked. Why had Zane tried to escape? Had he been brought to Narabia against his will?

Cat had wondered about the circumstances of his mother's decision to give up custody of her son. Zelda Mayhew Khan had fled Narabia not long after Zane's birth and taken him with her— the fairy-tale romance with the Sheikh obviously not living up to the media hype. The actress had never spoken publicly about her marriage and it seemed once she had faded from the public eye, she'd struggled to find work and had a string of arrests for DUIs and disorderly conduct when Zane was in his teens. So it had made sense Zane's father had assumed custody, but Cat had never been able to find a formal custody agreement—or a court order declaring Zelda an unfit mother—during her initial research. And she had wondered what it must have been like for a teenage boy, who had probably had minimal supervision while living with his mother, to suddenly find himself in a place like Narabia, where the customs and culture were a lot more constrained… But she hadn't suspected anything like this.

She was trying to formulate a question, keen to discover more about Zane's relationship with his father, when one of Nazarin's teenage granddaughters rushed into the tiny room at the back of her shop where they were talking.

'You must leave—the Sheikh, he comes on horseback with his men,' she beseeched Kasia and Cat in the native language.

'We should go,' Kasia said. 'He has come to find you.'

Cat's heart pummelled her chest.

Why had he come looking for her? And why did she have the feeling the answer to that question could not be good?

She didn't want to leave. There were so many questions she still had for Nazarin. But she could feel her granddaughter's fear and see Kasia's concerned expression. The last thing she wanted to do was cause any trouble for Nazarin, her family or Kasia. This could only be a misunderstanding. Yes, Zane had told her not to go anywhere unaccompanied, but she had Kasia with her. And anyway, she would have told him of this trip if he hadn't been so reluctant to talk to her.

Thanking Nazarin, she and Kasia left the room and hurried through the stall to the courtyard.

She pulled on her headscarf and shielded her eyes against the midday sun, which was blisteringly hot now. The spice market had closed an hour ago, the heat becoming unbearable, and the stalls had been packed away. Only a few people still milled around. But some of the citizens came out of their dwellings at the thunderous sound of hooves approaching.

Cat's breath clogged her lungs as six horsemen appeared on the ridge above the marketplace. Their shapes became distinct through the heat haze as they galloped into the courtyard. Out in front was a monstrous black stallion, the rider handling the powerful horse with consummate ease, his robes flying out behind him. He led the riders to a skidding stop in front of Cat and Kasia.

The stallion reared before his hooves crashed down only a few yards from Cat's toes. She scrambled back. Even with the traditional face and head covering she would have recognised Zane Khan anywhere.

It seemed the locals did too, because they were already falling to their knees in his presence,

Kasia included. Cat stayed upright, her whole body rigid with stunned disbelief, and something that felt suspiciously like awe.

Ripping off his face covering, Zane Khan leaned down towards her. His blue eyes glittered with temper, shocking Cat to her core.

Why did he look so furious?

The stallion pawed the ground as if mimicking its master's agitation as he held out a gloved hand. 'Up. Now.'

She probably should have taken his hand and done as he asked. She hadn't come to the market intending to anger him. She certainly hadn't thought he would come to fetch her back—after all, he had been too busy to even speak to her for over a fortnight.

But something inside her snapped at the autocratic command. She was here to do a job; what exactly was his problem with that?

'I'm not finished. I still have work to do here,' she said, clasping her hands behind her back.

Zane's curse was like a missile shot in the afternoon quiet and Cat cringed.

What was she doing? Perhaps she should do as she was told, and discuss this later, in a less public place? But before she'd had a chance to reconsider her position, he swung his leg over the saddle's pommel and jumped down.

He stepped closer, invading her personal space, towering over her, his big body positively vibrating with fury now. 'You're going to get on that damn horse without an argument,' he said in a voice low enough for only her to hear. 'Or there will be consequences.'

Mortification burned her cheeks and neck. But the desire to appease him and his temper vanished. She'd made her position clear, patiently and politely for two whole weeks—and she refused to be treated like a disobedient child for attempting to do her job.

'Stop bullying me,' she said, stiffening her spine. And refusing to show how intimidated she felt. 'I won't have it, just because I'm smaller and weaker and a lot less powerful than you are,' she added, keeping her voice calm and even—or as calm and even as she could while her heart was pounding against her ribs with more force than his horse's hooves. 'I came here to do a job—if that's not what you want you should never have hired me.'

His face hardened, a muscle in his cheek clenching so violently she was surprised he didn't dislocate his jaw. His eyes darkened to black, and his gaze swept over her, the heat in those deep blue eyes enough to incinerate every one of her nerve endings and make her pulse points pound.

Unbearable awareness rippled over her skin. His rich, enticing scent—soap and horse and musty male sweat—filled her senses, and desire shot through her, making her thighs loosen beneath the gossamer fabric of the robe.

Shock came first, followed by horrified confusion at her body's reaction.

What was happening? How could she be aroused by his outrageous behaviour? They were having an argument, for goodness' sake?

But then she saw the matching passion in his eyes, the brutal knowledge—and her confusion turned to panic. Could he sense her body's response?

'This isn't over,' he snarled, then bent and lifted her into his arms.

She gasped and had to grab his neck as he hoisted her up as if she weighed nothing at all and dumped her onto the horse's saddle. She grasped the pommel, the robe riding up to her knees as she straddled the wide leather, trying to prevent herself from slipping off the other side.

Her heart was hammering so hard now, she couldn't hear anything. The horse jolted and she squeezed her knees together, clinging on.

A large hand landed on the saddle in front of hers and Zane leapt up behind her in one fluid movement, landing at her back, his long legs and that enticing scent engulfing her.

The horse bucked and Cat let out a yelp.

'Easy, Pegasus,' he crooned, his breath hot at her earlobe as he banded his forearm around her waist, jerking her firmly into his lap.

Reaching around her, he grabbed the reins with the other hand and she became brutally aware of everywhere their bodies touched. His chest was a solid wall of muscle against her back, his thighs gripped her hips, keeping her anchored in place, and his groin pressed intimately against her bottom.

His size and strength felt overwhelming, almost as overwhelming as the brutal arousal that had sprung from nowhere—and which she seemed incapable of controlling. She watched in a trance as he yelled an order in Narabi and one of his men reached down to lift Kasia onto the back of his mount.

Suddenly Pegasus jerked forward and then

launched into a gallop. Her bottom bounced against the saddle, her heavy breasts pressed against Zane's forearm as he bent them low over the horse's neck and controlled the stallion with one hand. Her fingers gripped the Arabian saddle so hard she was sure she must be scoring the leather.

They shot upwards, climbing out of the marketplace. The enormous horse was surprisingly surefooted on the scrabble of sand and rock as they crested the rise and took the desert track back towards the palace, the walls looming like a great golden edifice in the distance.

Her world seemed to shrink to the pounding of the horse's hooves and the patient rise and fall of Zane's breathing and the jerky spasms of her own lungs as she tried to draw in a coherent breath. The desert track raced past so fast it felt as if they were flying, her body bombarded with sensation as every place he touched her burned hotter than the midday sun.

And the husky statement before he'd lifted her onto his horse began to play through her dazed and disorientated mind on a loop.

This isn't over.

While her confused, overloaded body tried to

figure out why the snarled words seemed more like a promise than a threat.

Zane was so angry by the time they reached the stables he could barely breathe, let alone think. And the few tortured breaths he could drag into his lungs were filled with the clean, refreshing scent of chamomile and honey.

He'd bullied and belittled her, and she'd called him out on it. But damn it, he had been terrified—that something might have happened to her. Thoughts of his mother and all the ways he'd failed her had been snapping at his heels as he'd ridden to the marketplace to find her.

And maybe he'd overreacted. But as they'd ridden back through the desert, her ripe curves bouncing in his arms, that provocative scent invading his senses, the struggle to bank his fear had become something a great deal more volatile.

Pegasus clattered to a stop in the yard, and one of the stable boys rushed forward to grab the reins. Zane disentangled himself from his passenger and dismounted. Holding her around the waist, he dragged her off the stallion. His temper spiked as he noticed the long robe, the hood dropping back to reveal her wild hair, which had been ruthlessly tied back to disguise her appearance from the guards, but was beginning to escape in tantalising tendrils.

Blood rushed to his groin and he cursed the effect she had on him.

The irrational fear got the better of him again.

She'd put herself in danger. Had deliberately disobeyed his orders. And then had the temerity to defy him when he'd arrived to see her safely back to the palace.

She clasped her arms around her waist, her gaze wary but direct as she watched him. As if waiting for him to explode again.

That she looked so wary but determined not to show it only infuriated him more.

He snagged her wrist, still too upset to speak, and hauled her out of the yard towards his private quarters.

'Where are we going?' she said, leaning back, trying to slow his steps.

He carried on walking. 'Somewhere private,' he managed around the huge boulder of barely suppressed fury, and something else, in his throat. He wasn't even sure any more if he was angry with her, or with himself.

At last they reached the doors to his quarters. He dismissed the guards outside.

He slammed the door behind them, his breathing so laboured he was surprised he didn't pass out. The effort to hold back his fear and his fury—and the dark tide of arousal—was almost more than he could bear.

'Don't ever leave the palace like that again,' he said, keeping his voice low so he didn't shout at her.

She flinched, but instead of backing down, instead of finally figuring out that this was no time to defy him, she did what she had done in the marketplace. She lifted her head, straightened her spine and thrust out her chin, the outline of her breasts heaving under the robe.

'Why not?'

'Because you are a woman alone in a strange country, and it's not safe. I would have thought that was obvious,' he said, his temper rising again. He rarely if ever had to explain himself. And he had no desire to explain himself now.

'I'm an academic. I have to be able to do the necessary research. And I wasn't alone. I was interviewing a seventy-year-old woman, with

Kasia's help. How could that possibly be dangerous?'

The bright flags of colour on her pale cheeks and the defiance in her eyes only made her more stunning.

She crossed her arms over her chest, her pulse battering her collarbone in hard heavy thuds. And he had the urge to place his lips against the pulse point and suck.

Focus, damn it.

'You are vulnerable. You should never have gone to the market with Kasia when you have no means of protecting yourself. You know nothing of our customs. Our culture.'

'And whose fault is that?' she said, her voice measured but firm, inflaming his already inflammatory temper even more. 'You brought me here to do a job but you won't let me do it.'

'I have arranged for you to see what you need to see,' he ground out, annoyed by the tiny note of defensiveness in his voice. 'With the proper protection.'

'No, you haven't, you've tried to micromanage what I see, and you've consistently refused to give me the access I need to your people. And even to yourself.' She hauled in a shaky breath.

'I'm beginning to think you're trying to hide something from me. That you never intended for me to write the truth.'

Because the accusation was astute and far too intuitive, damn her, he was forced to change his tack.

'The truth?' he snarled, his control snapping like a dry twig crushed under his boot. Desire pumped through his veins like wildfire. 'You're far too sheltered and naive to handle the truth about me and what I've been dreaming of doing to you for two solid weeks.'

The flush on her face rose to her hairline but instead of being cowed or appalled or disgusted with his revelation, as she should have been, her eyes darkened, the pupils dilating to black. And he had all the proof he needed that she was as fiercely aroused as he. Lust snapped and sizzled in the air around them, like a forest fire threatening to spark out of control.

'You've been dreaming about me?' she said, her voice a husky murmur of shock, which shouldn't have been at all provocative... But somehow it was, the curiosity in her tone as captivating as the artless arousal shadowing those wide caramel eyes.

'Yes, damn it,' he said, his own voice dropping to a broken hiss, ripe with the longing he could no longer disguise.

Heat seared Cat's insides. She shouldn't have asked him about his dreams; she shouldn't even want to know the answer... But her body—besieged by the pheromones that had brought it to wild vibrant life on the ride back from the marketplace—was in control now.

'I didn't know you'd been having them too.' She stumbled over the words.

He cursed softly, but then he gripped her arm and drew her against him. She felt the weight of his arousal pressing into her belly and passion flushed through her system. The musky male aroma of soap and the light, refreshing hint of cedarwood surrounded her. His knuckle touched her chin, and he lifted her gaze to his.

'And now you do,' he said.

She nodded, too overwhelmed by all the emotions and sensations bombarding her to speak. She'd surprised herself, by standing up to him, by letting him know how appalled she was by his behaviour in the marketplace.

But she didn't feel appalled any more. Not even

close. She felt excited, exhilarated and impossibly turned on.

The gossamer silk of her robe was like a straitjacket, her overloaded body yearning to tear it off and feel his touch on her naked flesh. No one had ever looked at her with such yearning. Such passion.

His thumb skimmed down the side of her cheek. 'I dreamt your skin was as soft as it looks,' he murmured. 'And I was right.'

His pupils darkened, filling the impossible blue of his irises. And the dangerous drawing sensation at her core dampened her panties. Her nipples drew into tight, aching peaks, her breath straining in her lungs.

He threaded his fingers into her hair and lifted her head. His lips brushed her mouth, but he didn't make the final move. And her dazed brain realised he was waiting, for her to make the choice.

All the reasons why she shouldn't kiss him flitted through her mind. But nothing could deny the hunger pulsing at her core.

Lifting on tiptoe, she clasped his waist and brought her lips to his.

His nostrils flared, like a stallion sensing

its mate. He said something under his breath in Narabi, the hoarse guttural murmur rasped across the swollen folds of her sex and then his tongue probed, licking across the seam of her mouth, demanding entry. Her breath gushed out as she opened to him.

It was all the permission he needed to take control of the kiss. His tongue thrust deep, exploiting her mouth in devastating, demanding strokes. She delved back, tasting him, tentative at first, but then finding a dangerous rhythm of thrust and counter-thrust. The burgeoning heat built into an inferno.

He ripped his lips away first, his breathing rasping in her ears, as his thumbs stroked her neck and he pressed his forehead to hers. Her back bumped against the carved wood of the chamber door.

'This isn't happening...' He groaned.

She wanted to contradict him, wanted to demand more—but as she clutched his shirt, her sex clenching and releasing with the desire to feel that massive erection inside her, all the reasons why they shouldn't be doing this came flooding back.

She jerked out of his embrace, the shame and

stupidity of what she'd done dousing her heated body like a bucket of icy water.

'I'm sorry. I didn't...' She stumbled to a stop, the futile excuses choking her.

She'd always assumed she was nothing like her mother, that she would never be ruled by her desires, never do anything foolish or reckless or selfish, simply to satisfy a physical urge. But now she'd done all three of those things and there was no excuse.

'I stepped over a line,' she said. 'I shouldn't have...'

'Shhh...' That treacherous thumb touched her cheek again, cutting her garbled excuses off at the knees. 'You didn't step over that line alone.'

Stepping away from her, he scrubbed his hands over his face. 'You should go.'

She nodded, understanding completely. She'd made a terrible mistake, and now she had to take responsibility for her actions...

'The p-project...?' she stuttered, distraught at the realisation she might have sacrificed her wonderful adventure for the fleeting pursuit of a hunger she didn't even understand.

'We can discuss it tomorrow,' he said. The

dismissal was clear and unequivocal. His tone strained.

A part of her knew she should be grateful.

He was allowing her to leave with her dignity intact. And when he tore up her contract tomorrow and sent her back to Cambridge, she would be able to kid herself at least some of her professional integrity was intact too. But as she fled back to the women's quarters she didn't feel grateful; all she felt was lost and confused, as the unrequited yearning continued to throb like a wound at her core.

CHAPTER FOUR

'I UNDERSTAND YOU asked to see me?' Cat said, all too aware of the hammer blows of her heartbeat as the door to the Sheikh's private office closed behind her.

Zane's gaze fixed on her, his devastatingly handsome face illuminated by the sunlight streaming through the window. His broad shoulders stretched the traditional tunic as he leaned back in his chair.

Potent, provocative and powerfully arousing, the sight of him reminded Cat far too forcefully of what they had shared only the day before.

Her breathing sounded loud in the strained silence. Too loud. Her thighs trembled. The proof that their one kiss still tormented her—as it had throughout the night—only made her more ashamed.

'You wanted an interview with me,' he said. 'I've decided to grant it.'

'You... What?' It was the very last thing she had expected him to say. She had spent the night fearing all the things he would say to her today. All the things he could accuse her of after sacrificing her principles and her objectivity the day before.

It had always been so easy for her to maintain her professional detachment before. But right from the start this project had been different. She'd become emotionally engaged, and now she was physically engaged too.

By the time Ravi had arrived to escort her to see Zane, she had been convinced she was coming here to get her matching orders.

'Y-you...' She stuttered to a halt, her emotions in turmoil. Again. 'You're going to give me the interview? *Now*, after... After what happened yesterday?'

'Yes.'

'But... But why?'

'Why not?' he said.

She pressed her hands to her sides, rubbing her sweating palms on the fabric of the robe, and forced herself to say it. 'Because we... We kissed each other.'

'I know we did.' His lips quirked, the sensual

smile making her hammering heartbeat plunge into her abdomen. 'Did you think I'd forgotten?'

She crossed her arms over her chest, then uncrossed them again, the reminder of how tender her breasts were not making her feel any less out of her depth. Any less compromised.

How could he be so nonchalant about this?

'No,' she said. 'It's just... I didn't think you'd want me to continue with the project.'

'Why not?' he said again, his pragmatism astounding her.

'For the project to have any credibility I have to be an objective observer,' she said. 'And now I'm not sure I can be. By kissing you I've compromised everything I—'

'Stop.' He held up his hand, cutting off her explanation with the arrogance of a man who had been born to make the rules, not to follow them. 'You're overreacting.'

'I... I am?' she asked, the blush burning her neck.

'It was a kiss, Catherine,' he said, as if he were describing something of no significance whatsoever. 'Nothing more. And it won't happen again. Of course you can still be objective. Now, do you want to continue with the project or not?'

'I...' She struggled, not sure what to say now. Or what to think. She'd convinced herself the answer should be no. But now he'd given her an option she hadn't expected she couldn't bring herself to say the word.

'Well?' he said, prodding her.

'Yes, I do want to continue with it,' she blurted out. 'I want to continue with it very much.'

Narabia's story would be a fascinating one to tell, and she already felt invested in being the person to tell it. But as he nodded, then swept out his hand to indicate the seat in front of his desk, she knew that wasn't the only reason she wanted to stay in Narabia. It wasn't just the mysteries of this beautiful country she wanted to uncover, but also the secrets of the man who ruled it.

'Then sit down and let's continue with it,' he said.

She forced herself to walk forward and take the seat he had indicated, trying to figure out if the line they'd crossed yesterday could now be uncrossed.

Perhaps her panic yesterday, all the shame and recriminations she had tortured herself with throughout the night, were simply a result of her chronic inexperience. She'd never been kissed by a man like that before, never felt that hunger, that depth of desire. But Zane obviously didn't think it was that big a deal.

Had she totally blown their kiss out of proportion? Because she had no frame of reference for these things?

'So, what is it you wanted to ask me?' he said.

He looked so calm, so confident, so implacable. The opposite of how she felt. But also the opposite of the man who had kissed her with such passion, such purpose yesterday afternoon.

Stop thinking about the kiss.

She flexed her fingers, then brushed her palms down her robe to steady herself. And regain at least a modicum of composure and professionalism.

She dragged out the notepad and pencil she kept in the pocket of her robe. It helped ground her as she flicked through the notes she'd made yesterday in the marketplace. She reread the questions she'd scribbled down before Zane and his men had arrived.

She cleared her throat, nerves assailing her. These *were* extremely personal questions, but surely he'd just given her his permission to ask them?

'I guess my first questions would be about how you came to be in Narabia when you were four-teen. Was there a custody hearing in LA, because I couldn't find any evidence of one? And did you get any say in the decision to transfer custody from your mother to your father?'

The muscle in Zane's jaw clenched, and his brows lifted. His expression became stormy and turbulent but the shadow of pain was clear and unequivocal before he had the chance to mask it.

Cat's insides clenched with the brutal sense of connection.

And she realised his reaction had already given her one of the answers she sought. To the question of whether she had any chance of rebuilding her objectivity after yesterday's kiss.

Because the answer was a categorical no.

Zane struggled to school his features... As his insides churned. And sweat gathered on his upper lip.

He'd woken up last night painfully aroused, the taste of her still on his lips. But as he'd lain in bed, staring at the ornate plasterwork on the ceiling of his bedchamber, he'd decided he didn't want Catherine to leave. He'd told himself it was because this project was too important. And he'd convinced himself he could control the hunger for her like everything else in his life. But now he wasn't so sure.

He'd decided to offer her the interview to re-establish clear boundaries. But now he could see he'd miscalculated. And he hadn't been entirely honest with himself.

What was the real reason he wanted her to stay? Was it really the project? Or the taste of her that he couldn't seem to forget?

And now this? Just when he thought he'd contained the problem, it had blown up in his face.

She was looking at him with sympathy and concern in her gaze. As if she could see inside his mind, and had already dragged out the answers he had no intention of giving her.

He wanted to halt her line of questioning, but in his arrogance he'd opened himself up to exactly this kind of intrusion. And now he could hardly shut her down without making it seem as if he had something to hide.

'The custody arrangements were agreed in private.' He swallowed, his throat raw as he tried to beat back the memories. 'My mother was...' He paused, knowing he would have to give Catherine something, even if every one of his instincts was rebelling at the thought of revealing even this much. 'She wasn't capable of handling me any longer. Like most teenage boys I was—' scared, lonely, confused '—unruly,' he managed. 'I needed a firm hand.' He shrugged, but the movement felt stiff and unconvincing, his back and shoulders stinging with the stark memory of the angry welts, the brutal pain that had been inflicted with so much relish. 'My father was able to supply the discipline she could not.'

'Were you happy here, when you first came to Narabia?' she asked, her voice soft and unthreatening, but ripe with compassion.

He stiffened. 'Of course,' he lied again, disgusted with himself now, not just for giving her the opportunity to ask the questions, but also for nearly giving in to the momentary urge to tell her the truth. 'But exactly how are my feelings as a boy relevant to this project?' he countered, going on the offensive.

She stared at her notepad, and the flush of colour spread out across her collarbone. But when she raised her head, he could see the compassion was still there.

To his shock he felt the jolt of awareness.

What the hell?

Nothing could have disturbed him more.

'Because in many ways your journey then is the same journey the outside world will experience now. Your story is the story of Narabia.'

'How?' he asked, disturbed now not just by the compassion in her voice, but the earnestness in her expression. She actually believed this nonsense.

'You spent the first fourteen years of your life living in the United States,' she explained, her tone rich with conviction. 'When you came here you couldn't possibly have been prepared for the immense cultural shift you would experience. Isn't this project about giving the outside world the same unique experience you had sixteen years ago? The chance to uncover the same secrets, to explore the same mysteries you found when you first came here?'

Absolutely not.

The thought horrified him.

The last thing he wanted was for the whole world to know the circumstance of his arrival in Narabia. But he steeled himself against letting his horror show.

The whole purpose of this project was to exorcise the pain, obscure the sordid truth and lock his past away in a place where no one would ever find it.

But as she stared at him, willing him to open up to her, he couldn't quite bring himself to stamp out the hope in her eyes.

'What I think,' he said, measuring his reply, 'is that it would be unwise to make me the focus of this project, Catherine.'

'Why?' she asked, still earnest, still convinced.

And he knew he would have to be ruthless after all.

Something was happening here that was a great deal more disturbing than that damn kiss. Something that could be a great deal more dangerous.

'Because people might question why you find my story so fascinating,' he said. 'Especially if they discover that your conduct here hasn't always been strictly professional.'

Blinking, she stiffened, the earnest expression turning to shame and humiliation as the delectable blush bloomed in her cheeks like a mushroom cloud.

'Yes, yes, of course.' She was clutching her

notebook so hard, he was surprised it didn't break in two. 'I see what you mean.'

He wasn't sure she really did see, because there was nothing more he wanted to do in that moment than finish what they had started the day before. Did she know she wasn't the only one struggling to maintain an appropriate distance?

He cut off the thought, forcing his mind, and his libido, back to the matter at hand—he needed to find a way to redirect her research and prevent her probing again into areas he couldn't let her go.

'You asked during our initial interview if you could review Narabia's ancient scrolls,' he said, seizing on a possible solution. 'I have asked Ravi to make them available to you.' He hadn't, but he would. 'They will make a much less compromising focus for your research.' The documents were the basis for the Narabian constitution, its ancient laws and customs. But there should be nothing in them that could feed back into the subject of his past.

'Oh, yes… That's…' She hesitated, her uncertainty strangely endearing.

He stifled the thought. He'd be wise not to mistake her honesty and transparency for harmlessness again.

'That would be very helpful,' she finally managed, her studied politeness doing nothing to mitigate the vivid blush running riot on her skin. 'Thank you. I look forward to reading them,' she added, but the passionate interest of moments before had dulled.

He tried not to regret it. With her searching questions, and her unsolicited sympathy, this woman had come closer than any of the women he had actually slept with to awakening needs which he'd thought he'd buried years before.

He couldn't risk having that happen again.

The kiss the day before was one thing. The chemistry they shared might well flare out of control again—and he wasn't quite as averse now to giving it free rein as he had been yesterday.

Physical desire, after all, was easily controlled, and easily forgotten once satisfied.

Catherine Smith captivated him, he might as well admit it—that fascinating mix of intelligence and innocence as irresistible as her live-wire response to his kisses. And she was going to be here for several months. The chances of them being able to keep a lid on the hunger that had flared so easily between them yesterday were slim to none, if he was being realistic. But before he let anything happen between them, he intended to be sure he could control the fallout.

He certainly could not allow her to get this close again to unmasking the weaknesses his father had worked so hard to kill—the neediness, the loneliness, the yearning for support and unconditional love that had crippled him as a boy—because they were the same weaknesses that had left him defenceless and had very nearly destroyed him sixteen years ago.

CHAPTER FIVE

CAT YAWNED AND rubbed her eyes, which had become gritty in the lamplight. Glancing up from the ancient transcripts, her tired gaze focused on the pale moon glittering through the geometric carvings on the shutters that shielded the library's precious documents from the outside.

Kasia lay on the divan opposite, having fallen asleep not long after they'd finished the evening meal served to them in the library's antechamber.

Cat stretched her neck, aware for the first time of the kinks that had set in while she'd been studying the scrolls.

She checked the time on her smartphone. Ten o'clock? Goodness, she'd been deciphering the ancient Narabian texts and jotting down notes on the origin of different customs and cultural norms for four hours straight without a break. No wonder her neck felt as if someone had tied it in a knot.

Pushing out a breath, she rolled the parchment, careful to overlay it with the linen used to absorb moisture, and tied it with the ribbon. Stacking it in the ornate chest, she sealed the lid and turned the key.

She'd been studying the scrolls for five days now. And had a wealth of notes to transcribe tomorrow in the office that had been set up for her in the women's quarters. But she'd done enough for tonight. Kasia needed her bed, and so did she.

After she'd woken her assistant—and friend—they made their way back through the labyrinth of corridors. Perhaps because Kasia had been half-asleep when they'd set off, after walking for twenty minutes, passing through several walled gardens and a series of covered walkways, Cat began to suspect they might have taken a wrong turn.

'Shouldn't we have reached the women's quarters by now?' she murmured.

Kasia turned in a circle. Two doors, one of which looked ornate and imposing decorated in hammered bronze, stood in front of them. Neither one looked familiar to Cat.

'I think we are lost...' Kasia confirmed Cat's fears, but then pointed to the more lavishly decorated door. 'But this looks interesting.' She tried the door, and it opened onto a flight of stairs. She smiled over her shoulder as she headed up the spiral staircase. 'Let us explore. This is part of the old palace—it will help with your research? No?'

'Wait, Kasia. We don't have permission to be here,' Cat whispered as she followed her friend. She didn't want to inadvertently incur Zane's anger again, especially given how that had ended the first time. In a kiss that she still hadn't been able to forget even after a whole week—during which she hadn't seen him once.

'If it was forbidden, the door would be locked,' Kasia whispered back, her shadowy figure disappearing round the curve in the staircase.

Cat raced to keep up with her, her footsteps echoing on the stone. They shouldn't be doing this. But she couldn't contain the shimmer of anticipation and curiosity—her fatigue forgotten—as they reached the top of the stairs and Kasia opened the door onto another chamber.

She heard Kasia catch her breath before she entered behind her.

Her own lungs ceased to function for two crucial seconds. Moonlight gilded the room in a silvery glow, but did nothing to disguise the staggering beauty of the gold-and-jewel-encrusted mosaic that covered the walls. A balcony looked onto a garden, the colours were muted in the darkness but the tinkle of water from the fountains and the heady perfume of the flowers convinced Cat it would look magnificent in the daylight.

Kasia flung her arms wide and twirled in a circle in the centre of the room, laughing softly. 'This is the Queen's salon. I have heard many tales of it, but I have never seen it for myself.'

'How do you know that?' Cat whispered, wishing Kasia would keep her voice down. Wasn't this private? They really shouldn't be here, she was sure of it now, even if the staggering artistry of the chamber was hard to resist.

'Because it is so beautiful,' Kasia said, as if it were obvious. 'Let's explore more.' Rushing to a dresser that stood against one wall, she switched on a lamp, casting a golden glow over the room.

Jewels sparkled and glowed, and dusty linens draped the furniture, which obviously hadn't been used for many years. But Cat couldn't help noticing the more modern touches. An old-fashioned record player stood on a book stand full of paperback novels, while a lavish couch was covered in a quilt with the Stars and Stripes on it, that looked incongruous next to the ornate Arabic-influenced interior design of the rest of the salon.

'Which queen did this place belong to?' Cat asked, but she already knew.

'Queen Zelda,' Kasia said, her footsteps soft on the silk rugs that covered the marble flooring as she rushed to an archway in the far wall and hauled back a screen. Her soft gasp propelled Cat across the room.

Kasia stood aside to reveal an array of silk robes, hanging in what had to be the Queen's dressing chamber. Made of gossamer-thin silk like the ones they both wore to stave off the heat, these lavishly embroidered garments had one crucial difference: the material was completely transparent.

Cat's cheeks heated as Kasia ran her hands under the cloth. 'Look how fine they are.'

Cat touched the silk, the fabric unbearably sensual against her fingertips. 'Do you know anything about Queen Zelda's time at the palace?'

It had never even occurred to her that Kasia might know something about Zane's mother.

Zelda had left Narabia when Zane was still a baby, which was over thirty years ago. Plus, the girl was an inveterate gossip, happy to give Cat the inside scoop on all the comings and goings of the women in the women's quarters, but she'd never spoken about the royal family. No one had.

Kasia looked sheepish. 'I only know the stories.'

'What stories?' Cat asked, dropping her voice to a whisper to match Kasia's furtive tone.

'They say that Tariq built this chamber for her when she became pregnant. He did not want her to drink the wine she loved too much. But when she became sad, he would not let her leave.'

'Are you saying he kept her here against her will?' Cat asked, unable to keep the shock from her voice.

Kasia nodded, avid curiosity lighting her face. 'Yes, that is what they say. That he kept her locked in here for many months, until the new Sheikh was born—like a beautiful bird in a gilded cage.' Kasia's florid imagery and her obvious eagerness to repeat the unsubstantiated gossip made the story sound preposterous. Like the plot of a trashy novel. Or a Gothic romance. But something about the chamber—its haunting beauty, the lingering scent of white musk perfume—felt oppressive… And desperately sad.

If Tariq had kept Zane here against his will as a teenager, wasn't it also possible he had kept his mother here against her will too? He would certainly have had the power to do so, if what she'd read in the ancient scrolls still held true today. That the Sheikh commanded a divine right to rule, not just over his subjects, but also over the royal household.

'That's tragic, if it's true,' Cat murmured. Maybe Tariq had been trying to save Zelda from her addiction, but he should have got her help, not just locked her up here. No wonder she had run away from him.

'No, no.' Kasia looked shocked by Cat's assessment. 'No, it is not tragic. It is romantic.' Kasia sighed and Cat realised in that moment how young and sheltered the girl was. 'Do you not see? He loved her with such passion, he could not let her go.'

'But she would have been a prisoner here,' Cat said.

Kasia only laughed. 'Would you not want to be a prisoner here—' she swept her hand out to encompass the stunning suite of rooms '—if you could have His Divine Majesty make love to you every night?'

Of course not, she wanted to say, but the denial got lodged in her throat, swallowed up by the wave of desire that had sprung from nowhere.

Heat rose up her torso, her nipples peaking painfully beneath her robe as the memory of Zane's lips feasting on her mouth blazed through her body like wildfire.

Oh, for pity's sake.

What was wrong with her? It had been a simple kiss. A mistake. They'd both agreed as much. Why couldn't she forget it?

Kasia lifted one of the negligees off the rail and held it in front of Cat.

'Imagine you are wearing this and the Sheikh comes to you,' she teased, batting her eyelashes outrageously. 'He is so handsome, and he wants only you. Would you say no?'

'Yes!' Cat croaked, wanting desperately to mean it, but the picture Kasia painted was all too reminiscent of the lurid pleasures that had chased her in dreams every night since she and Zane had shared that ill-advised kiss.

'Put it on. See how glorious it makes you feel.' Kasia grinned, the mischievous twinkle as enchanting as it was dangerous as she thrust the garment into Cat's hands. 'And then tell me you would turn the Sheikh away.'

The girl reached to undo the buttons on the front of Cat's robe.

'Stop it. Kasia! Are you mad?' Cat whispered furiously, finally managing to bat the girl's fingers away, but not before she'd undone enough buttons to have Cat's robe hanging open. 'I'm not putting it on. That would be totally wrong.'

'I know. I was only joking.' The girl pressed a hand to her lips to contain her laughter. 'But you looked so shocked. I could not help teasing you.'

And then the strangest thing happened: Cat's huff of outrage broke out of her mouth in a giggle.

She shouldn't find this funny, because it absolutely wasn't funny. At all. But as Kasia's laughter joined hers—echoing off the chamber's lush furnishings—Cat felt something let go inside her. Like a lock clicking open, releasing all the tension and turmoil that had been tormenting her for days. Until all that was left was the absurdity of the whole situation.

More chuckles popped out—until she and

Kasia were bent over, tears of laughter streaming down their faces.

Cat gasped for breath and felt the warm glow
of kinship. A kinship she'd never had before.

As a schoolgirl, and later in college, she'd always been so serious, so sensible, concentrating
on her work, and making a point of not asso-
ciating with the frivolous, fun girls, girls like
Kasia—full of life and mischief and spontane-
ity—because she'd been fearful of having too
much fun, and being distracted from her studies. But as she and Kasia laughed together the
thought of being lost in the Sheikh's palace and
discovering this treasure trove of impossibly
erotic outfits became more ridiculous and ri-
otously funny by the second—and it occurred
to her how much she'd missed out on. Because
somehow or other, she'd found such a friend in
Kasia.

'What's going on in here?' a deep voice demanded.

Cat spun round so fast she almost fell over.
The last of her laughter got trapped in her lungs,
swallowed by shock.

Kasia went deathly quiet beside her, then
dropped to her knees.

'Your Divine Majesty, please forgive us,' her friend murmured, her forehead touching the floor in supplication. She sounded terrified.

Zane Khan stood on the balcony, his arms folded over his chest, his big frame leaning negligently against the carved wooden rail, watching them.

Mortification flushed through Cat's system.

Oh, good grief, how much had he seen...? And heard? Exactly how long had he been standing there?

'Please accept our deepest apologies, Your Excellency,' Kasia mumbled, her voice trembling now like the rest of her. 'I will accept any punishment you deem fit.'

'It's not Kasia's fault.' Cat finally found her voice, concerned herself now. He hadn't moved, and it was impossible to read his expression. Was that amusement she could see or annoyance? 'It's totally my fault. I take full responsibility.'

They'd trespassed in his dead mother's salon. Touched her clothing.

Horrified at the sudden realisation she was still clutching the sensual silk to her breast, she jerked both hands behind her back.

'I see,' he said as he pushed off against the rail

and strolled into the room. His gaze remained fixed on her face—which felt as if it had heated to about a thousand degrees. 'Then I'm afraid one of you will definitely have to be punished.'

Could she hear the hint of humour? Or was she imagining it?

'Then punish me,' she said, knowing she couldn't take the chance he wasn't joking. 'Not Kasia.'

'Okay,' he said, and she saw it then, the glint of humour.

She should have been relieved. He wasn't mad, he appeared to be amused. But as he continued to walk towards her, his presence sucked all the oxygen out of her lungs, and all the tension that had been tormenting her for days screamed back across her shoulder blades.

She was trapped by her own acute awareness of him, her whole body responding in ways she knew it shouldn't to his nearness. His enticing scent intoxicated her as he stopped in front of her, and touched her flaming cheek with the side of his thumb.

'Kasia, you may return to the women's quarters,' he said without looking at the girl as he dismissed her. 'And mention this to no one.'

'Yes, Your Divine Majesty.'

Trapped in Zane's gaze, Cat heard the relief in the girl's voice—and the hint of humour—before her footsteps disappeared and the door slammed behind her.

Cat's blush hit critical mass. Was it obvious? Even to Kasia? Her reaction to Zane?

'I'm sorry. We shouldn't have come in here, I…'

He touched a finger to her lips, silencing the rambling apology. 'Don't…' he said, the husky smile in his voice weakening her knees. 'It was good to hear laughter in this room for once.'

She wondered what he meant, but her curiosity died, washed away on a wave of longing when he ran his thumb down her neck, and brushed the pulse point hammering against her throat. Flattening his other hand against her body, he ran it down her side and curled his fingers into the material at her waist, tugging her towards him.

'Breathe, Catherine,' he said. And the breath she didn't know she'd been holding gushed out. 'So *would* you?' he asked.

'Would I what?' she repeated dully.

'Would you turn the Sheikh away? If he wanted only you?'

His deep voice, raw with need, made Kasia's teasing words sound provocative, potent, thick with desire—and nothing like a joke.

Her answer got trapped in her throat. Something hard brushed against her hip. Entirely of its own accord, her gaze drifted down.

The loose tunic and pants should have hidden a lot, but they couldn't hide *that*. She stared at the prominent outline of his erection. His knuckle touched her chin, lifting her traitorous gaze back to his face.

'Do you like what you see, Catherine?' he asked.

She nodded, slowly, the raw need in his voice mesmerising her and making the melting sensation in her panties all the more intense. She should stop this, leave now, before they did something they would both regret. But she was trapped by the need too, to feel his sensual lips on hers again. And everywhere else her body burned for his touch.

His fingers flexed and he yanked her closer still. Until she could feel his penis trapped against her belly.

Her breasts swelled against her bra as his gaze slid over the sensitised skin of her cleavage, exposed by the buttons Kasia had undone.

Arousal flared in the depths of his irises and coloured his skin.

'Please...' The raw need in her tone echoed around the room.

Bending his head, he planted his lips on the pounding pulse in her neck—and sucked.

Hunger powered through her, and her head dropped back, giving him better access, her pulse roaring where his lips feasted.

'Zane...' she cried, the sob of need becoming a plea.

'Yes, I know,' he muttered, his voice a broken whisper.

And just like that, the dam of longing she'd been keeping so carefully leashed for the past week broke and the devastating tide of yearning rolled through her like a tsunami. She lifted shaking fingers and plunged them into his short hair as she dragged his head up.

She wanted his lips on hers again. Wanted to feel that exhilarating jolt of passion, of freedom.

As if he had heard her secret desire, he slanted his mouth across hers. He feasted on her mouth, exploring the recesses, tempting and torturing her, swallowing her sobs. Her fingers massaged his scalp, running over the bones of his skull, rejoicing in the coarse silk of his hair.

He lifted his head, those intense blue eyes boring into hers in the shadowy light. 'I want you so damn much. Tell me you want this, too?'

That he would ask, with such desperation in his voice, spoke to something inside her, tapping a spring she hadn't even known existed. It geysered up and burst out of her mouth.

'Yes… Yes, I do.'

He scooped her into his arms and carried her out onto the balcony.

'Where…? Where are you taking me?' she said, the nerves twisting to life in her stomach.

They shouldn't be doing this.

'To my chambers,' he said as he marched along the balcony and entered another suite of rooms. 'As good as it was to hear laughter in my mother's salon,' he said, carrying her through an outer chamber into a lavish bedroom suite, 'I'm not about to make love to you in her bed.'

Make love to you.

The words seemed to echo in Cat's soul. Romantic. Forceful. Her foolish heart sped up into overdrive.

That's not what he means.

They didn't love each other. They hardly knew each other. This was about sex. About basic elemental attraction, but still her galloping heart slowed, and her limbs softened.

An imposing four-poster bed stood on a raised podium; golden drapes hung from the frame. Arched windows looked down into the private garden, the perfume of exotic blooms and the sweet spice of lemons drifting in on a midnight breeze.

But Cat could barely register any of it, her system already overloaded with sensations. The bulge of muscle and sinew beneath her bottom, the scent of his skin, salt and cedarwood, the ragged tenor of his breathing. Placing her on her feet, he dealt with the rest of the buttons on her robe in seconds and shoved the garment off her shoulders. The silk pooled at her feet.

She stood shivering in the fragrant night air, aware of the confining lingerie as his gaze devoured every inch of her flesh. She crossed her arms over her chest.

'Don't,' he said, the tortured rasp torn from his

throat. His gaze met hers, dark with lust. 'Don't cover yourself,' he demanded. 'You're exquisite.'

She forced herself to release her hold on her shoulders, to bring her arms to her sides, to let him look his fill—even though it terrified her. No man had ever seen her with so few clothes on before.

But no man had ever called her exquisite before either.

She jolted, shocked by his touch as his palm covered one of her breasts, and he drew his thumb across the straining nipple. The subtle caress sent fire shooting down to her core. With a deft flick of his wrist, the front hook of her bra released with a sharp snap.

She shuddered as he peeled the lace back. He held her naked breasts in his palms, let the calloused skin cup the underside, as if testing the weight, then circled the aching tips with his thumbs.

A deep moan burst from her throat as he plucked and tugged, playing with the nipples, making the ache in her sex sharpen and spread.

'Beautiful,' he said. Then he bent to capture one swollen nipple between his teeth.

The maelstrom of need fired through her as his

hot, avid mouth closed over the peak and suckled hard. She gripped his head, the drawing sensation too much and yet not enough, as liquid need welled at her core.

Her knees shook, her thighs became liquid. He stopped, then lifted her in his strong arms again and laid her on the bed.

He kicked off his boots. The dull thud as they hit the floor, first one, then the other, echoed in her head. She watched, transfixed as he untied the band on his tunic, let the loose pants fall over long, lean legs. The muscles in his thighs bunched, and she noticed the thick bulge beneath the cotton. Lifting up on her knees, she gathered the hem and lifted the tunic to reveal the strident erection.

He was large, and long, much larger than she had expected, even after feeling that thick ridge against her belly.

'Can I...?' She glanced up. 'Can I touch it?' she asked, hopelessly unsure.

His teeth flashed white in his face.

'Sure,' he said.

She trailed her finger up the swollen length, her teeth sinking into her bottom lip. Her thumb glided across the top, spreading the bead of moisture over the broad purple head.

'Stop.' He snagged her wrist and dragged her hand away.

'I'm sorry,' she said. 'Did I do something wrong?'

He kissed the tips of her fingers. 'The only thing you keep doing wrong is apologising for nothing.'

He climbed on the bed, supporting her as she lay down. His lips found her pebbled nipples—and her mortification dissolved on a wave of desire.

She bucked off the bed as he licked across her ribs, circled her belly button, then pressed his face into the lace covering her sex.

She wanted him to take off the tunic, she wanted to see all of him, but her voice was locked somewhere in her chest, too scared to demand anything in case she broke the spell. The clamour of need rushed through her limbs, and melted her core as he sank his teeth into the delicate lace of her panties.

The sound of rending fabric filled the room as he ripped the fabric away.

She fisted her fingers in the sheets, trying to

cling to her sanity, as he cupped her buttocks in firm hands and held her open for his mouth.

'You smell incredible,' he said. 'I want to taste you.'

It sounded more like a demand than a request, but still she nodded.

The blush suffused her whole body, when his deep chuckle reverberated up from her core.

And then she launched off the bed, her hips nearly bucking him off as his rough tongue swiped through the slick folds.

He held her hips, his fingers digging into her flesh to hold her steady for the delicious torture. She panted and sobbed as he swirled his tongue everywhere but where she needed it the most.

She writhed, tortured by the devious darts and licks. The coil of sensation twisted tighter and tighter, until she was moaning, begging, sobbing.

'Easy, Catherine,' he murmured and she was reminded of the way he had handled his horse.

Animal instincts drove her—she needed that thick length inside her. She felt so empty, her sex clenching in a desperate desire to be filled.

He eased one thick finger into her sex, then two, stretching the tight flesh, and finally fastened his lips on the very heart of her, flicking his tongue in a driving, relentless rhythm.

She screamed, her voice so hoarse she didn't even recognise it. Her back bowed, her body thrusting into his mouth, her fingers fisting as the ruthless orgasm fired from her core and burned through her body in one mind-blowing wave of pure unadulterated pleasure.

He licked her through it, drawing out every last drop of sensation.

She sank back onto the bed, exhausted, limp and uncoordinated.

Rearing over her, he tugged off the tunic and flung it away. Her vision filled with the magnificent sight of bronzed muscle, and the happy trail of hair bisecting his six-pack.

Grasping her legs in unsteady hands, he looked savage, feral as he angled her hips and notched the head of his erection at her core.

He pressed in, slowly at first, but, even with the slickness of her orgasm easing the way, the stretched feeling inched towards pain.

She clutched his shoulders, determined to bear it, wanting more. Wanting all of him. But her fingertips slipped on the slick skin and she felt a series of ridges as her fingers glided over his back.

He was punished harshly for his disobedience.

Compassion assailed her as Nazarin's words drifted through her mind but then he thrust hard, lodging the thick length deep inside her.

She cried out in pain, and his head reared up.

'Catherine?' He stilled, his expression tormented. 'Are you a virgin?'

'No,' she said. She hadn't meant to lie, but she didn't want him to stop, scared she would never again feel the dizzying pleasure that lurked so close.

'It's okay,' she said.

He eased out, then rocked back to the hilt. The brutally stretched feeling began to ease, the ripples of pleasure rising from her core, then getting stronger, more relentless as he established a devastating rhythm.

The orgasm built again, slowly, surely, robbing her of breath. She sobbed, her fingers digging into his shoulders as his movements became wild and uncontrolled.

He swelled inside her, and her muscles contracted, sending her over the edge. Pleasure pulsated through her body, her wild cries matched by his harsh shouts as he wrenched out of her and hot seed splashed onto her belly.

It took her a while to come back to her senses, her whole body shuddering with the force of her climax, and his.

So that's what all the fuss is about?

The inane thought spun through her head as he rolled onto his back and drew her with him.

She lay sprawled over his body, her soft curves flattened over hard contours. Her legs tangled with his, her cheek resting on his shoulder, while his thumb drew lazy circles on her back.

She rose up on one elbow to look into his face—usually so harsh, for once his expression looked relaxed, long dark eyelashes resting on his cheeks. He opened one eye and the sensual line of his lips tipped up in a disarming smile.

Her ribs tightened, her heart thundering in her chest. She was glad she'd made him smile; he really didn't smile nearly often enough.

The magnitude of what they'd done seemed worth it for that smile.

'I hope you feel suitably punished,' he murmured, and she felt her own lips quirk—even though her chest felt unbearably tight.

His hand cupped her cheek, and he swept her hair behind one ear. 'What is it?' he said, concern shadowing his eyes. 'You look worried.'

How did he read her so easily? When she found it next to impossible to read him?

'What did you mean, when you said it was good to hear laughter in that room?' she asked.

His fingers stilled in her hair, and she wished she could take the impulsive question back.

'I'm sorry. I shouldn't have asked that, it's not relevant to the—'

'Now, don't start apologising for nothing again,' he said and continued playing with her hair.

There was no edge to his voice, the tone relaxed, but she suddenly felt hideously exposed. The fog of afterglow finally clearing from her dazed brain and making her realise exactly what she'd done.

The project? Her contract? If she thought a kiss had compromised that, what about falling into bed with the Sheikh?

Sitting up, she grabbed the sheet to cover her breasts and felt the slight soreness where he'd reddened the areolas with his kisses.

'Hey,' he said as she scooted off the bed. 'What are you doing?'

She leaned over the edge to locate her robe. 'I

should go back to the women's quarters. I need to pack.'

She could feel tears stinging the backs of her eyes.

What had she done? She'd really messed up this time. This wasn't just a mistake. It was a catastrophe.

She spotted the edge of her robe under the bed, but as she leaned over further to pick it up the sheet around her body tightened and she couldn't budge.

'Why do you have to pack?'

She glanced over her shoulder, to see him propped up on one elbow, his fist gripping the other end of the sheet and preventing her from moving.

'Because I have to leave. Obviously. I can't possibly stay here after what just happened.' She tugged on the sheet, knowing she was becoming hysterical but not quite able to stem the flow of feelings. She was her mother's daughter after all. 'Zane, please let go.'

'No way,' he said. 'Not until you stop talking garbage. We slept together, Catherine. It was good. And kind of inevitable after that kiss.'

Was it?

She wanted to argue with him, appalled by his casual response to actions that had put the whole project in jeopardy.

'I… I still can't stay,' she stuttered, desperate to tug the sheet out of his grip.

The blush fired up her chest. The last thing she needed right now was to have to wrestle with him.

Then he gave the sheet a sharp yank and she collapsed against his chest.

He clasped her round the waist and kissed the top of her shoulder blade as she tried to squirm away from him. 'Calm down, Catherine… You're overreacting again.'

He suddenly stilled, the low curse startling her as he let her go.

'What the hell is this…?'

Taking her chance, she scrambled off the bed, but as she turned back to him, the sheet now wrapped securely around her, she could see what he was staring at.

The flecks of her blood on the bottom sheet.

His gaze rose to hers; the colour had drained out of his face. 'Is this menstrual blood?'

She could have lied to him again. But she wasn't a dishonest person. And the words simply wouldn't leave her lips. Her face flushed with guilt in the tractor beam of his gaze and she was forced to shake her head.

'You lied?' he said. 'You *were* a virgin.'

'I didn't mean to lie… I just didn't want you to stop,' she said.

'Did I hurt you?' he said.

'Not really,' she said, the concern in his words striking right at the heart of all her insecurities. That it would matter to him, that he would care, felt huge when she knew it shouldn't.

'It's a yes-or-no answer, Catherine,' he said, his eyes dark with a torment she didn't understand.

'It only hurt for a moment. Then it felt very good.'

He nodded and then looked away. She took the opportunity to slip the robe back on, her body trembling with reaction, the sore spot between her thighs beginning to throb.

They'd just made love… He'd given her her first—and then her second—proper orgasm. But it had meant much more to her than it should—which had to be why this conversation felt far too intimate.

His jaw clenched, the tension in the hard muscles of his chest suggesting that he wanted to say something. For the first time he looked frustrated. Maybe he was annoyed with her after all. But he didn't say anything and, as always, it was hard for her to tell what he was thinking.

Although she suspected it was probably along the same lines as what she was thinking. That this had been a very bad idea.

'Do you need me to escort you back to the women's quarters?' he asked.

The dismissal felt like a blow. But she tried hard not to let the hurt show. She shook her head, scared she would give herself away if she spoke.

He pointed to a door on the opposite side of the chamber. 'If you leave through there, one of the guards can show you the way.'

'Okay,' she managed past the boulder of grief in her throat, for all she'd lost— No, not lost... Thrown so carelessly away.

'We can talk more about the repercussions of this tomorrow,' he said, not unkindly. But still she felt compromised, and wobbly and hopelessly exposed.

She nodded, her throat raw.

Because what could there possibly be left to talk about now?

CHAPTER SIX

'YOU CANNOT LEAVE, CATHERINE.' Zane watched Catherine's face flame, her eyes full of humiliation. And confusion.

'But surely I must. I can't possibly continue with the project if—'

'Please let me finish.' He held up his hand, struggling to control the swift kick of temper... And frustration.

He should not have touched her. Should not have given in to the hunger that had flared as soon as he'd heard her laughter coming from his mother's old chamber. Because the possible repercussions of her innocence would now force his hand. And hers.

'The project can continue,' he said. She opened her mouth to deny this claim. 'But the project is the very least of my concerns at this point.'

'It is?' She seemed astonished—and he wondered, not for the first time, why she put so little value on herself. She was a vibrant, beautiful woman; she'd given herself to him with no restraint, no hesitation last night. But he had seduced her. Not the other way around.

'Certain facts from last night need to be addressed.' He watched her response carefully, some of his anger dissipating when her brows launched up her forehead.

'What facts?' Either she was a better actress than his mother, or she was genuinely confused. The bitter cynicism tying his guts in knots began to ease. Whatever else this was, it hadn't been a set-up.

'In your research,' he asked, because he needed to be sure, 'did you read anything about the Laws of Marriage for the Sheikh?'

She shook her head, her glorious eyes widening.

'You were untouched. As the Sheikh, if I take a woman to my bed who has never before known a man, Narabian law requires me to marry her and honour her as my Queen. It is an ancient tradition—brought in many centuries ago—to protect young girls in the Sheikh's palace from being exploited.'

'But I'm not that young, and you didn't exploit

me. You didn't even know I was a virgin,' she said, sounding a little frantic now.

The frustration flared. Which made no sense at all. He did not want to be forced into a marriage any more than she did.

'The fact though remains that you were one.'

'I'm so sorry I lied. I shouldn't have lied to you. It was stupid and selfish and shameful and—'

'Catherine, please stop,' he said, cutting off the guilt-ridden monologue as he got up from behind his desk and crossed the office.

She sat, staring at her hands, which were clutched tightly enough in her lap to whiten her knuckles. Kneeling in front of her, he covered her hands with his.

'I've ruined everything, haven't I?' she said, her voice so forlorn he wanted to sweep her up in his arms again.

Not smart.

He resisted the impulse. Getting any more intimate with this woman would be a mistake. She'd already had an unpredictable effect on him. Because it wasn't just ancient Narabian law that made him want to protect her from the consequences of their actions.

He nudged her chin up with his index finger.

'Listen to me, Catherine. You were not the only one in that room last night. And you weren't the one with experience of these matters. I was.'

'Yes, but I'm the only one who lied,' she said. 'And now you're in a massive constitutional bind because of me.' She blinked furiously, and he felt the deep pang under his breastbone at the misery sheening her eyes.

How ironic was it that it had been seeing her in his mother's salon—so sweet and open and artlessly arousing—that had made it impossible for him to deny his desire any longer?

He knew the stories about that chamber. That it had been a prison. That his father had locked his mother in there when she became pregnant with him. He had no idea whether those stories were true, because it had upset his mother too much to talk about his father when she was sober.

He suspected the truth was less lurid, and more complex though, because the only time his mother had talked about his father—when she'd been the worse for drink—she had always insisted Tariq had been the only man she had ever loved. And that she had never been able to forget him.

Something he had never understood. How

could his mother continue to care for a man whose love, whether real or imagined, had eventually destroyed her?

Or rather, he had never understood it, until now.

He didn't love Catherine. And he wasn't about to fall in love with her. He had promised himself long ago he would never allow himself to be damaged by love the way his mother had. Love was a destructive force, because it required the loss of self. And whatever love his mother had still felt for his father, he'd had no delusions about how his father had felt about her, once he'd been brought to the palace.

But he could see how easily an intense physical attraction—such as the one he and Catherine shared—could mess with your head. And all your priorities. Or he wouldn't be kneeling in front of her now, desperate to take the misery out of her eyes.

'We should be able to ignore the constitutional bind on two conditions,' he said.

Catherine's head shot up. 'We can? Oh, thank goodness.'

Her profound relief kicked at his pride. He

clenched his teeth, determined to ignore the contrary reaction.

'What are the conditions?' she asked, the eagerness in her voice prodding at his composure.

'That your virgin state last night doesn't become common knowledge,' he said, something he'd already taken steps to control, by asking Ravi to burn the bed sheets and having a confidential word with Kasia not to spread news of their liaison. 'And that there are no unforeseen consequences.' Which was by far the more problematic detail.

'Unforeseen consequences? You mean if I get pregnant?' she asked, the turmoil in her face becoming more acute.

'Yes. I didn't use any protection,' he said. 'Are you by any chance on the pill?'

Zane didn't look angry, he just looked troubled. But still Cat felt the tension in her stomach tighten, and the misery caused by this conversation threatened to engulf her.

How could she have been so reckless? So impulsive? She hadn't even considered contraception until this moment. Heat blazed across her cheeks and she was forced to shake her head.

He swore softly under his breath.

'I... I should have said something,' she stammered. How could she have got so swept up in the moment that she hadn't considered the risk of pregnancy? Perhaps because she'd been far too busy worrying about her position at the palace, and the feelings that Zane had aroused ever since she'd met him, to worry about anything else.

'I'm not sure I gave you a chance,' he murmured.

'I'm sure I won't get pregnant,' she said, trying to right this situation. 'I had my period only a few days ago. I'm nowhere near the middle of my cycle.'

He nodded, but he didn't look entirely convinced. 'That's something, I guess.'

'And you pulled out,' she said, remembering the seed she had washed off her stomach as soon as she'd returned to the women's quarters. 'I'm sure the chances are very slim. But maybe I could take emergency contraception?'

He shook his head. 'Such options are illegal in Narabia. It would cause an uproar if the people believed you were trying to prevent a pregnancy.'

Cat could well imagine; having discovered the power of the Sheikh after studying the ancient scrolls, she knew the Sheikh was treated like a living god.

'I'm afraid the Sheikh's seed is considered sacred,' he murmured, the wry smile disconcerting but also comforting. Apparently, he didn't blame her for this disastrous turn of events—even if she was not going to be able to stop blaming herself. 'Stopping it finding fertile ground would be considered a capital offence.' He continued, 'Do you wish to return to the UK?'

She shook her head, the impulse instant and unequivocal. 'No, I think… The chances are so slim… I really don't think it's necessary.'

He nodded. 'Good. Then we are agreed.'

That he was happy for her to stay, despite everything, seemed huge. But as he walked back to his desk and took his intoxicating scent with him, regret pulsed low in her abdomen.

She stifled the ludicrous reaction. Hadn't her foolish pheromones got her in enough trouble already?

'We shall continue with the project as normal,' he added, sitting back down behind his desk. 'If you fled the country now, there would be questions about why, and then keeping the truth of what happened last night under wraps would be even harder.'

She nodded, the rush of joy ridiculous in the circumstances, but there nonetheless. She'd been convinced she would be returning home today. And while the reasons why she would have to stay were hardly ideal, she was still glad she didn't have to leave Narabia.

The memory of Zane's lips on the yearning spot between her thighs, the sound of lace ripping, had the febrile heat flushing through her system.

She squirmed and squeezed her thighs together, but could do nothing to stop the flood of warmth.

'Catherine? What's your answer?'

She looked up to find Zane watching her, with the same intensity with which he had watched her last night.

'I'm sorry. Did you say something?' she said, realising he must have been talking and she hadn't been listening.

His gaze narrowed, searing her skin. The warmth glowed between her clenched thighs like molten lava, doing nothing to make this situation any less mortifying.

'I am taking a trip to visit the Kholadi chief, Kasim, tomorrow. Would you like to accompany me? They are Narabia's only remaining nomadic tribespeople and such a trip will help re-establish your reasons for being in this country.'

Her sex pulsed hard, at the thought of accompanying him...anywhere. 'Yes, that would...' She cleared her throat, her voice distressingly husky. Like that of a lover. Which of course she was not. Or not any more. 'That would be very useful.' She stood. 'Thank you, for being so reasonable about all this.'

'Catherine, wait...'

She turned from the door, unnerved as he crossed the room.

'You mustn't blame yourself for something I was a great deal more responsible for than you,' he said.

He was being generous. Far too generous, really. She shouldn't have lied to him about her inexperience. But even though she knew that, her frantic heartbeat slowed at the understanding in his eyes.

'Are we clear on that?' he prompted.

She nodded, too emotional to speak.

'Good.' He touched his thumb to a lock of hair.

'I will have the necessary garments sent to you for tomorrow's trip.' He tucked the errant tendril back behind her ear, and then thrust his hand into the pocket of his trousers. The shimmer of sensation ran down her neck and tightened her nipples. 'It will be a hot journey and you'll have to wear the full veil while we travel.'

'To observe the traditions of the nomadic tribespeople?' she asked.

'No.' His lips tipped up on one side. 'To stop your skin from being fried to a crisp.'

She nodded, not trusting herself to speak. Then left the room on unsteady legs, the tug of intimacy at his familiar caress and the protective comment crucifying her. But as she hurried back to the women's quarters, determined to read up on all the information she had on Narabia's nomadic tribes in preparation for the trip, so they could both re-establish the distance they had so comprehensively lost, it wasn't caution and concern that dominated her thoughts, but the dangerous burst of longing.

CHAPTER SEVEN

'YOUR EXCELLENCY, I'M SORRY, but I think there's been a mistake.'

Zane glanced round from adjusting the stirrup on his saddle, to find Catherine standing behind him in the stable yard. He steeled himself against the familiar surge of arousal at his first sight of her since yesterday in his office. Even with the ankle-length black riding robe draped over her, he could still imagine the abundant curves beneath. Could still capture her scent in his memory—fresh and spicy and so seductive. Could still see the wonder in her eyes when she'd looked at him, touched him.

He'd invited her on this day trip to the Kholadi Oasis in Narabia's desert lands on the spur of the moment yesterday. He'd persuaded himself at the time it was because they needed to re-establish a professional distance between them. But now he wasn't so sure.

He still wanted her. Too much.

Making the impromptu invitation, and the motives behind it, indulgent at best—and dangerous at worst.

He faced her. 'You can call me Zane, Catherine,' he said, attempting to quell his annoyance at the formal address.

Even if they weren't going to repeat the folly of two nights ago, he was still responsible for her, until they had established she was not carrying his child.

And whatever the outcome of that situation, he would always be her first. She'd made the decision to give him her virginity, without telling him, so she had no right to expect him to simply dismiss that as if it were of no consequence. He didn't believe it was of no consequence to her and it certainly wasn't to him.

She hadn't fastened the veil sewn into the robe's headdress over her face yet, giving him a clear view of the light flush on her cheeks.

'I'm not sure calling you Zane is appropriate,' she said. 'Won't it seem a bit disrespectful in public?'

'I decide what's disrespectful and what's not,' he said, letting his frustration show. 'I've felt your body clench around me while you climax,' he added, under his breath so only she could hear him. 'I think we can safely say that calling me Zane is not going to be more inappropriate than that.'

She blinked and the blush fired over her face, illuminating that tempting trail of freckles across her nose. 'Yes—yes, of course,' she said, frustrating him even more, because now he felt like a bully.

'You said there's been a mistake? What mistake?' he asked, trying to moderate his tone. What was wrong with him? Goading her wasn't going to make this situation any easier to bear, or any less volatile. Quite the contrary.

'The horse,' she said and pointed towards the Arabian mare that he had arranged for her to ride after a lengthy discussion that morning with his stable manager, Omar.

'What's the problem with the horse? Zakar is small, I know, but she is one of our finest mares, very docile and amenable.' He'd had it on good authority from Omar—after quizzing the man for twenty minutes. It was only a four-hour ride to the oasis, but he wanted to ensure Catherine would be safe and not overtaxed. He had already informed his men they would be taking a more circuitous route to avoid any terrain that might be too challenging for their guest.

'It's not the horse, exactly. She's beautiful,' she said. 'It's just…' She hesitated and chewed her bottom lip. The urge to touch his tongue to the reddened skin and soothe the place where her teeth sank into it had his frustration levels increasing.

'It's just what?' he snapped. And she stopped biting her lip. Thank God.

'It's just that I don't know how to ride her,' she said, the blush flaring again.

'You don't ride?' he said, his frustration dissolving at the look of embarrassment on her face.

She shook her head.

'But you sat on the horse very well when we rode back together from the marketplace.' Her body had moulded to his as they'd galloped back to the palace. Far too well in fact, because having her in his arms, moving in unison with him, feeling her muscles tense and release, her breasts plump against his forearm, had been one of the most arousing experiences he'd ever had—until he'd got her naked in his bed.

'You're kidding,' she said. 'I was sure I must

have felt to you like having to ride a horse while holding onto a sack of potatoes.'

Despite his frustration, and the vision now clouding his brain of her body cradled against his, he had the strangest urge to laugh at the look of total astonishment on her face.

'I assure you,' he said, his voice a barely audible rasp, 'nothing could have felt less like a sack of potatoes.' He cleared his throat, the urge to laugh comprehensively destroyed by the renewed urge to take her in his arms again and ride her, instead of letting her ride Zakar.

'Are you telling me you've never ridden a horse before that? Ever?' he asked, struggling to quell the desire threatening to run riot again.

'No, never.' She looked concerned, her teeth tugging on her lip again.

He groaned inwardly. The spike of heat to his groin was not welcome.

'Could I drive to the location instead?' she asked.

'The Kholadi live in the desert. It is not possible to drive all the way to the oasis.'

Her face fell. 'I suppose I can't go, then,' she said.

He clicked his fingers and one of the young

stable lads rushed forward to serve him. 'Fit Pegasus with the larger saddle,' he said in Narabi to the boy. 'And tell Ravi to arrange for a car to transport Dr Smith to Allani.'

He turned back to Catherine. 'I have arranged for an SUV to take you from here to the end of the desert road in Allani. We will rendezvous there and then you will have to ride with me the rest of the way to the oasis.'

Her eyes popped open, wary and concerned, the flush of awareness riding high on her cheeks. 'Won't that be too much for the horse?' she said.

'Pegasus is a big horse.' He let his gaze glide down her frame. 'You are a small woman. And we will only be sharing the mount for an hour. The stallion will be fine,' he said, although he wasn't sure why he was so determined not to leave her behind.

He decided not to examine the decision too closely.

Three hours later though, as the lush curves of her breasts settled against his forearm, her bottom tensed between his thighs and her agonising scent filled his nostrils, it occurred to him he might have made another serious error in judgement—as all the blood in his brain surged south.

* * *

The shimmer of impossibly blue water in the valley below, shaded by a grove of palm trees and edged by an encampment of at least a hundred tents, looked like an optical illusion to Cat as Pegasus trotted over the crest of the dunes. Or something created by a particularly cruel CGI artist. She sucked in a breath, the cloying cloth of her veil sticking to her dry lips. Zane's arms tightened under her breasts, as he shouted something in Narabi to his men.

The order was followed by a series of whooping shouts and suddenly she was forced back into Zane's embrace as he spurred Pegasus into a full gallop down the side of the dunes. The horses' hooves made dull thuds in the solid sand, and her body jumped and jiggled, the soreness in her thighs and bottom nothing compared to the riot of sensation that had been driving her wild for what felt like days now.

The ride had been arduous. Within ten seconds of mounting the stallion in front of Zane, his big body surrounding her, Catherine had questioned the wisdom of agreeing to ride with him.

She should have made her excuses. And stayed at the palace.

This promised to be a fascinating trip—she'd been able to find out next to nothing on the Kholadi and their chief, other than that Kasim was the youngest chief the Kholadi had ever had, and he'd spent his early years living at the palace. Interviewing him would add considerable weight to her study of Narabian society. But she was so tired and sore now, and overstimulated, she had lost the ability to care about anything but getting off the horse.

Far more arduous than the ride had been the enforced proximity to Zane. And she was certain he'd found it just as arduous. Because she'd felt him tense whenever her bottom had shifted in the saddle or his forearm had tightened around her midriff.

And even worse than the physical proximity had been the thoughts and feelings that had spun through her tired mind without warning, as the stark beauty of the desert landscape had brought her emotions far too close to the surface.

She should have spent the journey thinking of her research protocol, what she wanted to learn from this visit. Instead of which she'd been fixated on every minute movement of his body behind hers, and the devastating erotic memories of what they'd shared and would never share again.

As the oasis spread out before them, the inviting water the same translucent blue as Zane's eyes, a group of heavily armed Kholadi tribesmen appeared from the main tent in the enclosure to greet them. One man stood out, a head taller than the other tribesmen—at least as tall as Zane. Cat guessed he must be the chief from the sabres he wore and the gold braiding on his dark robes, which glittered in the sunlight.

Shots were fired into the air by the other tribesmen—the deafening pops of gunfire combined with the deep guttural whoops of Zane's men.

Cat clung to the saddle as Zane dismounted. Unlike the rest of Narabia's citizens, the Kholadi tribesmen showed none of the same deference to Zane, several of them patting him on the back. Zane made his way towards the man she assumed must be Kasim. They clasped hands and then drew together in a hug. The chief clapped Zane's shoulder and said something in a dialect Cat didn't understand.

As the bodyguards led the other horses away, she was left sitting on Pegasus, not sure whether to attempt to dismount on her own, as Zane and the Kholadi chief appeared to be deep in conversation. When suddenly all eyes, including Zane's and the chief's, were directed her way.

Hot and sweaty and sore under the cloying fabric of the riding robe, she had never felt more self-conscious in her life. Then the chief said something in the same incomprehensible Kholadi dialect and a round of loud laughs and guffaws ensued.

Zane stiffened and she could see his displeasure at the comment as he strode towards her. 'Come, I will introduce you to Kasim.'

'What did he say?' she asked.

She stifled the blush that wanted to heat her skin. If she got any hotter she'd pass out. And fainting would only make her humiliation and misery complete.

'Nothing important,' Zane said, but she could hear the snap of irritation in his tone as he gripped her waist. Grasping his shoulders, she let him lift her off Pegasus's back. But as her feet touched the sand, her knees buckled.

Zane banded an arm around her waist, keeping her upright. 'Are you okay?' he demanded, his voice thick with concern. 'Do you need me to carry you?'

'No, no, please. I'm fine, I'm just a bit stiff.'
She'd die of embarrassment if he carried her.

'I should never have expected you to ride so
long without a break,' Zane said, the concern in
his voice making the sensation in her stomach
dip.

Don't read anything into it.

She forced herself to walk, stifling the groan
of pain as her thigh muscles protested.

As they approached the chief together, the
young man smiled, startling her a little. He had
the same striking bone structure as Zane, even
though his skin was several shades darker and
his eyes so brown they were almost black.

'Kasim, this is Dr Catherine Smith. She is a
Middle Eastern scholar from the UK. And she is
going to write a book about our country,' Zane
introduced her, placing a possessive hand on her
back. 'Treat her with the proper respect.'

The Kholadi chief laughed, his eyes twinkling
with mischief. A silent communication passed
between him and Zane—which made Zane tense
and Kasim's grin widen. Whatever Kasim had
said about her a moment ago, she would hazard
a guess it had nothing to do with her academic
qualifications. She should have been insulted,

but she was charmed instead when Kasim gathered her fingers and made an extravagant production of kissing her knuckles.

'The Kholadi are honoured to have His Divine Majesty's woman in our humble camp,' he said.

His woman? Is it that obvious?

'Oh, I'm not… I'm just an academic,' she sputtered, struggling to come up with a convincing denial while her exhausted body replayed the wonder of being Zane's woman for one night.

'There is no *just*, when a woman is as beautiful as you,' the Kholadi chief declared.

Don't blush. Please don't blush.

Heat exploded in her cheeks, and Kasim's lips quirked with a wealth of knowledge.

Oh, for goodness' sake, why don't you just wear a sign saying Zane's Woman Here?

'Behave yourself, Kasim,' Zane said—the warning tone as tense as she now felt. 'Dr Smith needs to freshen up and then she would like to talk to you about her research. Do you have a tent she can use?'

'Of course, brother,' Kasim said, but the mocking light turning his eyes a rich chocolate brown suggested he wasn't chastened in the least.

The two men exchanged a few more words

in the Kholadi dialect before Kasim ordered a young woman to escort them both to a large tent situated on a small hill at the top of the encampment. Cat had no idea what the men had said to each other, but as Zane cupped her elbow and directed her through the camp she could tell his temper was being held at bay with an effort.

'Kasim seems like a nice man,' she said in a desperate attempt to break the tension.

'The one thing Kasim is not is nice,' he snapped, the temper now vibrating through his voice. 'Don't be fooled by that thin veneer of charm. The man is a goddamn...' He stopped talking, and Cat glanced at him, disturbed by the stormy expression.

'The man is a what?'

'Nothing,' he said as he lifted the tent flap and held it open for her to walk inside. Whatever he had been going to say, he'd obviously thought better of it.

But still Cat wondered. Was there bad blood between Zane and the Kholadi chieftain? Kasim had seemed relaxed and friendly, but Zane looked murderous.

'Why did he call you brother?' she asked, intrigued by the casual form of address.

Everyone else treated Zane with such deference, but Kasim treated him very much like an equal.

Zane scowled down at her. But didn't reply.

Then two women appeared, bareheaded and with a number of piercings in their brows and noses, their flowing robes made of fine silks. They fell to their knees in front of Zane. He spoke to them in rapid Kholadi. And then directed Cat into the main area of the tent.

Cat gasped. It was like walking into a cave of wonders, the bold colours and luxurious furnishings in stark contrast to the austere outer appearance of the dwelling.

A carved wooden bed on a platform stood in one corner covered in richly embroidered pillows. Thick, elaborately embroidered rugs covered the floor and velvet curtains had been drawn back to reveal a gleaming copper tub in the opposite corner surrounded by low tables piled high with linen clothes and an assortment of small glass bottles. The scent of perfumes and incense filled the surprisingly cool and refreshing air inside the tent.

Zane led her to a large divan draped in luxurious silk and directed her to sit down. Cat winced as her abused buttocks made contact with the pillows.

'How bad is it?' Zane asked.

'Not too bad,' she lied as she tried to shift into a more comfortable position. If only she could stand up but she wasn't convinced her legs would hold her upright, because the walk across camp had turned them to putty again.

Leaning down, Zane touched his finger to her nose and smiled, the crinkle of his lips both strained and yet sympathetic.

'These two will look after you. I've told them to feed you and then give you a long hot bath. After that they'll give you a massage. It will be sore as hell at first, but the oils and ointments they use will make it feel much better once they're done.' His voice seemed to sink several octaves as he described the massage—putting her overstimulated nerve endings even more on edge. He straightened. 'I'll come back to get you, once you've had a chance to rest. We've been invited to join Kasim for supper. He will answer any questions you have about the Kholadis' way of life.'

He turned to leave so abruptly she shifted to

grab his sleeve. And hissed as the pain shot up her thigh. 'Wait, Zane.'

He stopped, but the way his gaze tracked to where her fingers touched his forearm had her releasing his sleeve immediately.

'What is it, Catherine?' he said, the patience gone again. He was angry about something, but she had no idea what.

'Won't it be dark by then?'

'I expect so. What's your point?' he replied.

'Is it safe to make the return journey at night?'

As much as she didn't want to have to get back on the horse, she *really* didn't think she could get back on it in the dark. And not just because of her abused butt muscles. But because she didn't think she could spend another hour cocooned in Zane's arms while the darkness increased the intimacy... Or she was liable to lose what little was left of her sanity.

Zane's gaze remained steady on hers for two pregnant beats. 'You're in no condition to ride again tonight,' he said. 'We'll have to stay here overnight. And return to the palace tomorrow morning.'

'Oh...' she said, both relieved and yet somehow more wary. Was this why he was so annoyed?

Because she'd turned out to be so feeble? And why was his grudging concern making her stomach muscles melt?

'Don't freak out, Catherine. We won't be sharing the same tent,' he said, the tension snapping in his voice again.

But I wasn't worried about that.

'I'll be back to get you in a couple of hours,' he continued. 'Get as much rest as you can.'

She nodded, then flopped back on the divan as his heavy footfalls left the tent. Now more confused and wary than ever.

Because the thought of sharing a tent with him had not bothered her at all. And it really should have. Especially as the last thing she needed right now was to ride anything else.

'I discovered from my research that you spent your early years at the Sheikh's palace. Why was that? And why did you leave?' Cat asked, her curiosity about Kasim's past getting the better of her as his servants removed the empty dishes they had been feasting on for the past two hours.

The Kholadi chief had been vocal and engaging throughout the lavish meal. She'd feared he might be as evasive as Zane, but he'd been the opposite, regaling Cat with stories of how he had come to assume the chiefdom—a series of trials by combat against the other young men in the camp after the previous chief had died without a son. She'd quizzed him about the Kholadis' customs and culture and he'd answered every inquiry, even offering to translate any conversations she might want to have with his tribespeople.

The food had been delicious. They'd eaten with their fingers, a lavish banquet spread out on the low tables. After the soothing bath and massage, the aches and pains of the ride had been forgotten while she lounged on the bed of cushions, chatting with the Kholadi chief and devouring exquisite dishes heavily spiced with Middle Eastern flavours. The low lighting had added a spellbinding intimacy to the proceedings.

The only dark spot had been Zane, who had sat stiffly and stony-faced throughout their discussion. Cat tried to ignore him. He was obviously annoyed at having to stay overnight, but this interview was providing her with exactly the sort of information that would give her study context and authenticity. The Kholadi had been a closed community, its culture virtually unknown to the outside world. And Kasim was a fascinating and captivating host.

Even though they weren't drinking any alcohol, she had become a bit dazed. But the minute she had asked the question about Kasim's past at the palace, she realised her mistake.

A tense silence descended, the convivial atmosphere in the tent vanishing as Kasim's gaze connected with Zane's over her head.

Had she said something wrong?

'You don't have to answer that,' she said, backtracking. She hadn't meant to impose on Kasim's hospitality. She should never have asked him such a personal question.

But then Kasim's gaze tracked to hers, and his teeth flashed white in his dark face in the familiar charming smile. The mocking light had reappeared in his eyes. 'Zane has not told you?'

'Told me what?' she asked, detecting an edge to his tone that belied the amused expression.

'It's not relevant to the project, Kasim,' Zane interrupted them, his voice gruff with warning.

But Kasim ignored the warning. 'The answer to your question is a simple one, Dr Smith. I lived in the palace as a boy, because I was the old Sheikh's bastard son.'

Kasim was Zane's brother!

Cat dropped the pencil, her fingers going numb as she did a double take between Zane and Kasim. It seemed so obvious now, the striking similarities between their features, why Kasim had called him brother when they arrived. It wasn't some special form of tribal address. They *were* brothers. Or rather half-brothers.

Why hadn't Zane told her when she'd asked? And why did he look so angry now?

'My mother was a Kholadi prostitute. She died giving birth to me,' Kasim continued as Zane swore softly.

'You're not putting that in the damn book,' Zane told her, his voice curt.

'Of course,' Cat said. 'I won't put anything in there that—'

'I am not ashamed of my origins, brother,' Kasim interrupted her. His wide lips had drawn into a tight line, the relaxed smile gone, as he glared at his brother. For the first time, he looked as tense and annoyed as Zane. 'Why should you be?'

'Damn it, Kasim, you know that's not it,' Zane said as the tension snapped between them.

Standing up, Zane reached down and helped

Cat to her feet. 'I need to have a conversation with Kasim in private,' he said, the muscle in his jaw working overtime. 'It's time you went to bed.'

She nodded, feeling hideously responsible for the tension. 'I'll go back to the tent.'

Kasim stood too. 'There is no need for her to go,' he said.

'It's okay, Kasim. I'm exhausted anyway,' she said, desperately trying to smooth over the argument that seemed to be brewing between the two men... The two brothers. 'Thank you so much for a marvellous meal. And for your invaluable help with my research.'

Kasim watched her for a moment, then nodded. He escorted her to the entrance to the tent, making a point of leaving Zane behind them.

He whispered instructions in Kholadi to a burly man dressed in traditional garb.

'Ajmal will escort you to your sleeping quarters,' he said before bowing over her hand to kiss her fingers again. 'It was my great pleasure to meet you, Dr Smith.' The warmth in his eyes suggested he wasn't just being polite.

'I'm so sorry if I caused a problem...' She could see Zane bristling, his stance rigid with annoyance as he stood back, waiting for Kasim to bid her goodbye.

'You are not the cause of this problem,' Kasim murmured, but the twinkle of amusement had returned to his dark eyes. He bowed again. 'I must return to my brother before he threatens to kill me for spending too long with his woman.'

'But I'm not...' Cat began, but Kasim had already left her standing in the doorway to the tent.

His woman.

Ajmal led her back through the camp, to the tent she had left earlier, the two handmaidens appeared to help her prepare for bed. She dismissed them, feeling too agitated for company, and donned the exquisite sleeping robe they'd left out for her, which turned out to be completely transparent.

Thank goodness I'm not sharing a tent with Zane.

But as she drew the curtains closed around the tent's bed and lay on the mass of pillows, the events of the evening kept running through her head.

If only she hadn't given in to her curiosity and asked that personal question.

But why had Zane reacted so violently to Kasim's announcement? Surely he couldn't be ashamed of being Kasim's brother? From everything she'd learned about Zane during her time at the palace, he treated his staff and his subjects as equals, not subordinates. He wasn't a snob. And it was clear there was a bond between the two men. They had greeted each other warmly when she and Zane had arrived.

She watched the torchlight flicker and glow through the bed's curtains, the scent of incense drifting on the cooler night air, and tried to still her thoughts. But then her hand strayed to her belly, sliding over the thin silk.

What if Zane's baby is growing inside me?

A heavy weight crushed her lungs, making it hard for her to draw a breath. What would she do? She didn't know if she could be a mother, and she certainly didn't want to become one in these circumstances. So why did the possibility not feel like as much of a catastrophe as it should?

She forced her hand away from her flat stomach.

Get real, Cat. You're not pregnant. You're just tired and out of sorts after the long ride and the extremely tense end to the meal with Kasim.

Zane and the Kholadi chieftain would thrash out whatever had been bothering them and that would be the end of it. None of it was her business, because she wasn't Zane's woman. End of.

But as she drifted off to sleep Kasim's words echoed in her head—over and over again—and, unlike yesterday, when the thought of being pregnant with Zane's child had filled her with raw panic, now all it did was make the sweet spot between her thighs throb, and the hollow, empty space in her stomach glow.

Damn Kasim—the man was an inveterate flirt.

Zane cursed his half-brother and the loss of temper that had led to an hour-long stand-off between the two of them after Catherine had left them.

He glanced up at the glittering canopy of star-light above his head, and let out a heavy sigh as he made his way back through the camp. After an hour spent with her pert bottom wedged between his thighs was it any surprise he'd had a major sense of humour failure during Kasim's charm offensive?

Catherine had lapped up the attention. But he could hardly blame her for that. The fact he hadn't been able to tell Kasim, in no uncertain terms, to back the hell off hadn't helped with his frustration.

He'd been forced to watch the two of them while he choked down the evening meal, and tried not to give free rein to a jealousy he knew he shouldn't be feeling. But damn it, the woman had come apart in his arms less than forty-eight hours ago. She might even now be pregnant with his child. Having to watch his half-brother hit on her had been the last straw after a whole hour of feeling each slight shift of her body and not being able to do what he wanted to do.

Was it any surprise he'd been furious with Kasim?

Especially as he had no doubt Kasim had known exactly what he was doing. His half-brother was a bastard in more ways than one.

He checked the knee-jerk thought.

Kasim's legitimacy, or lack of it, had never come between them before tonight. Had never been a part of their relationship. He'd made sure of it once his father had relinquished his grip on the throne and he'd finally made peace with the Kholadi, or rather their young chieftain. The boy his father had cast out of the palace without a backward glance when he'd installed Zane as his reluctant heir.

Neither one of them had had a choice back then, both forced to be part of their father's machinations. He'd worked long and hard to persuade Kasim they were brothers, that whatever had happened back then had not been his choice. And he'd nearly blown five years of diplomacy to smithereens tonight because of jealousy—over a woman of all things.

He nodded to the guards on the outside of the tent where he always stayed when visiting the Kholadi.

The scent of jasmine and lemons filled the air, reminding him of when he'd left Catherine here earlier. He pictured her being bathed and massaged by two of Kasim's servant girls. The familiar arousal pounded to life in his pants.

Stop thinking about her, naked and yearning. You ordered her sent to another tent. Precisely because you're not going to give in to the lust again.

Not only that, but he'd just spent the last hour insisting to Kasim that Catherine wasn't his woman. Which had made it even harder to ex-

plain away his snarky response when Kasim had
revealed their sibling relationship.

During the evening, he'd dug himself into a
hole. And it had taken him over an hour to dig
himself out of it again. The fact he'd got the defi-
nite impression Kasim had been enjoying baiting
him for the last thirty minutes or so—once Zane
had convinced him his surly behaviour had nothing to do with Kasim being the son of a prostitute—hadn't exactly helped him to relax.

And now he was wound tighter than a damn
spring.

*You tell me she is not your woman, brother.
And yet you look at her like a starving man.*

The whole evening had been some weird
power play on Kasim's part. He was sure of it—
because, despite all the charm and convivial-
ity, the brotherly bonhomie, Zane knew the guy
still held a grudge for the appalling way he'd
been treated by their father. That Zane didn't
blame him for that though, wasn't making him
feel any less pissed with his half-brother about
the way Kasim had used Catherine to get a rise
out of him.

She was inexperienced, wholly unaware of her
own charms and she didn't know she was being

played by a serial womaniser to make him jealous. For that transgression alone Zane had been hard-pressed not to punch his half-brother's lights out. But he'd been forced to sit on his hands all evening, pretending it didn't matter, forced to disguise the fact that Catherine *was* his woman. Or had been.

He crossed to the bathing area to rinse his face and noticed the copper tub was still full of water, probably from Catherine's bath that afternoon. The scent that had clung to her filled the air.

His groin throbbed like a sore tooth. And he knew the deep dreamless sleep he needed before the torture of tomorrow's return journey was likely to elude him.

Damn Kasim. And damn Catherine for being so alluring without even trying.

The blood throbbed painfully in his groin, so he stripped off his clothes and stepped into the tub. He gathered a cloth and sluiced his aching body with the cool water. Unfortunately the water wasn't cold enough to deflate the rampant erection.

Taking the rigid flesh in hand, he began to pump the hard shaft in fast, efficient strokes—

while struggling not to imagine the woman he couldn't even claim as his servicing him instead.

Cat shivered awake to the sound of movement in the tent. A cooling breeze whispered across her skin, but heat engulfed her body—as if in an erotic dream—as she heard the splash of water and…a muffled grunt.

Was someone in the tent with her?

Still groggy with sleep and the myriad erotic memories that had pursued her in dreams, she leaned over on her elbows and drew back the curtain.

Her gaze drifted to the far corner of the room—and her breathing stopped, squeezed to a standstill in her tortured lungs, as every one of her pulse points thudded in unison.

I'm still dreaming. I must be.

The soft shimmer of torchlight caressed Zane's tall muscular form as he stood in the tub, completely naked, facing her, water glistening on the defined contours of his chest and legs. But instead of bathing himself, he held his iron-hard erection in his fist, his fingers gliding over the solid column in a fast, relentless rhythm.

Blood powered into Cat's clitoris, making it

swell and ache, and moisture flooded between her thighs.

He looked magnificent, his skin given a golden glow, the trail of hair across his chest tapering into a line through the bunched muscles of his six-pack and then blooming into a thicket at his groin, where his penis stood, thick and proud.

She watched him pleasure himself in rough strokes. His body bowed back, the guttural moan rasping deep in her own sex as he reached his peak.

His breathing deepened, the rigid lines of his body softening.

She shifted on the bed, trapped in an erotic trance. The fine silk of the sleeping robe slid over her skin like sandpaper, her own body still fraught with arousal. She breathed, mesmerised by the far-too-graphic dream, as Zane picked a cloth up from the water and washed his genitals.

The splash of water sounded so lifelike, the sensation prickling over her skin felt so vivid, the scent of jasmine incense and woodsmoke smelled so distinct.

How can this dream be so real? Why don't I want to wake up?

But then he dropped the washcloth and swung

round to lift one of the linen towels by the tub and the torchlight illuminated his back.

The erotic dream evaporated as she took in the ragged scars marring the smooth skin.

Her breath guttered out on a harsh sob of distress, which sounded deafening in the heavy silence.

Zane jerked round and their gazes locked.

The erotic tension snapped tight in her abdomen.

'Catherine, what the hell are you doing in my bed?' he rasped.

Not a dream. Her mind screamed but still the hunger built like an inferno. The sheer fabric rubbed against her nipples, and she suddenly became far too aware of the sight she must make to him in the transparent robe. All her senses on high alert.

She scrambled to lift the sheet and cover her nakedness.

'I… This is where Ajmal told me to sleep,' she managed to get out round the shock thickening her throat.

The swell of emotion at the sight of his ruined back combined with the deep throbbing in her sex to leave her feeling raw and exposed and far too needy.

Zane swore, hooking the linen towel around his nakedness. 'I'm going to murder Kasim.'

Had Kasim planned this? But why would he do that...?

'He didn't believe us when we said we weren't a couple?' she asked.

'It doesn't matter what he believed,' Zane snarled, sounding furious with the Kholadi chieftain. 'He had no right to treat you with such disrespect.' Marching across the room, he began to pick up the clothing he must have discarded.

'When I get hold of him, he's a dead man,' he said.

Before she could think better of the impulse, Cat dropped the sheet and scrambled off the bed.

'Zane, don't.' She caught his arm, her heart breaking all over again at the sight of those terrible scars.

Was this the punishment Nazarin had told her about? How could his father have done such a thing? What kind of a man would treat his own child with such brutality?

'You need to let go,' he rasped, the words burning with intensity and barely controlled passion.

Cat's pulse leapt as she released his arm, but the need to soothe the fury tightening his features remained. 'Please don't be angry with him. It doesn't matter.'

'How do you figure that?' he said, his face tight with temper. 'He's insulted you, by placing you in my bed as if you're a concubine. Damn it, he probably told the servants to give you that robe. Look at it—you're practically naked. And after I specifically told him more than once that you weren't here to warm my bed, you were here to research a book.'

She could feel his gaze through the transparent silk, making her skin prickle and hum with awareness.

She needed to tell him the truth, however compromising it was. She cleared her throat. Trying to find the words. 'Maybe he didn't mean it as an insult.'

What Kasim had done had clearly compromised her and on one level she did feel insulted. But Zane's furious defence of her honour was making her feel something else entirely.

'I wouldn't be so sure,' Zane snarled.

'And maybe I'm slightly responsible for this,' she offered.

His gaze bored into her before he ran his fingers through the short damp strands of his hair and looked away. 'How the hell could you be to blame for this, Catherine?' he asked. 'You're letting that bastard off the hook far too easily.'

She swallowed. She could lie to him, end this conversation now—let him leave and blame Kasim for the heat powering through her system—and dispel the brutal feeling of intimacy. But she couldn't make herself do it.

If nothing else she needed to be honest about her own desires. She'd convinced herself she'd come on this trip to enhance her research. But the truth was a lot more complicated.

'I still desire you,' she murmured. 'Even though I know I shouldn't.'

Zane hadn't said anything, so she forced herself to continue.

'I came on this trip because I wanted to be with you. If Kasim arranged for me to be brought to your bed, maybe he only did it because I wasn't able to hide how much I still want you.'

Zane turned, his naked chest gleaming in the torchlight, his breathing rough as he looked at her at last. Then he lifted his hand, and cupped her cheek. 'Damn it, Catherine, don't say stuff like that.'

She leaned into his palm. 'Why not, if it's the truth?'

'You're leaving yourself defenceless. Don't you get that? You've already given me too much. You need to protect yourself. I'm not a kind man, or a good one.'

Yes, you are, or why would you care whether I'd been insulted by your brother?

His gaze sank to her abdomen. 'If you turn out to be pregnant, if anyone discovers you were a virgin…you'll be forced to marry me. And I won't do a damn thing to protect you. Because I'm as ruthless as my father was.'

She shook her head. 'But I'm not pregnant. And no one's going to discover I was a virgin. And it's just the two of us here…' She moistened her lips, gratified when his gaze shifted to her mouth, and his pupils darkened to black. 'Maybe we should view Kasim's trick as a gift. Rather than an insult.'

She didn't want to create even more friction between the two men. But she wasn't being self-less now, she was being selfish.

Why couldn't they have one more night? As long as they were careful.

She could smell soap on him and the scent of leather, and feel her heart pounding in strong, steady thuds.

Taking his hand in hers, she placed it over her breast. The nipple pebbled instantly through the transparent robe.

'What are you doing?' he asked, attempting to tug his hand away.

'I want you tonight, Zane. If we can enjoy each other without risking pregnancy, why don't we?'

They both wanted this. Why should they deny it?

His palm caressed her nipple, the calluses teasing the sensitive tip into a hard peak. 'Are you sure?'

'Yes, I am.' She'd never been more sure about anything in her life. Their first time had been a result of incendiary sexual chemistry. But this felt more intimate, more honest. She wanted to own her desire for him. To finally expel all the guilt she'd felt about her mother's actions.

Grunting, he captured her other breast.

The surge of relief was almost as huge as the

surge of excitement when his thumbs circled the engorged peaks.

'I'm still going to kill Kasim,' he muttered, but then he bent to lift her into his arms.

He carried her to the bed and dropped her on the pile of pillows, then climbed up and caged her in. The robe had fallen open to reveal one breast; he fastened hungry lips to the responsive peak. She bucked, a ragged moan issuing from her lips at the drawing sensation in her core. The sound of rending silk tore through the staggered sound of their breathing as he ripped the robe apart and laid her bare.

Her body trembled with sensation, her throat closing on emotion as she plunged her fingers into his hair and he pressed the heel of his palm between her legs. He watched her, his blue gaze wild, feral, as he eased first one finger, then two into her sex.

'You're still so tight,' he murmured. 'I don't want to hurt you.'

'You won't,' she said. 'What should I do?' she asked.

'How much did you see, earlier?' he said, working her swollen flesh and finding the stiff nub at the top of her sex with his thumb.

'Everything,' she said, her voice hoarse with longing as she moved against the tantalising caress.

He huffed a laugh, then took her hand and placed it on the thick erection. 'Hold me,' he said.

She curled her fingers around him and caressed him in tentative strokes, rejoicing as the firm flesh leapt and throbbed against her palm.

'Slow down, or I'm not going to last long.' He groaned, pressing his face into her hair.

They lay together, teasing, tempting, torturing, learning each other's responses, learning just where and how to touch to bring joy.

She cried out, lifting up to meet the thick thrust of his fingers, desperate to feel that final oblivion. Her nails scored the ruined skin of his back as he rocked into her hand and he massaged the walls of her sex with his touch, nudging a place so deep inside she panted in desperation.

She clung to the high wide plain of pleasure, her fingers slipping on his sweat-slicked skin as he forced her over that final edge.

The wave of pleasure broke over her, and she heard him shout out against her neck, then tense as his seed splashed against her belly.

She lay for what felt like hours, holding his

head against her neck, running her fingers through his hair. Trying to pull back the emotions unleashed by their coupling and bury them deep.

Just sex. Only sex. Don't go there. You can't afford to make this more than that.

Eventually Zane raised his head. 'Maybe I won't kill Kasim after all.'

She smiled, or tried to, the pulse of emotion making it hard for her to speak.

She felt cold and strangely bereft as he levered himself off the bed and walked back over to the copper tub. The torchlight limed the smooth muscular line of his body and flickered over the scars—which seemed as much a part of him as the proud tilt of his head, and the powerful bunch of his biceps.

He returned with a wet cloth and proceeded to wipe his seed off her belly. Then he delved between her legs, gently cleaning the oversensitive folds. She lay patiently, letting him take care of her, her whole body shuddering, as she tried not to make too much of his tenderness.

Zane was a conscientious and pragmatic man. He probably treated Pegasus the same way after a hard ride, she thought, then winced at the realisation she'd just managed to compare herself to his horse. But the foolish thought had the desired effect, locking the unnecessary emotions back where they belonged when he threw the cloth away and climbed into the bed with her.

He dragged her into his arms, and held her close. He didn't say anything, but she felt the intimacy of what they'd shared like a heavy blanket, binding them together as she listened to his breathing in the semi-darkness.

'Did your father give you those terrible scars, Zane?' she murmured, unable to hold back the need to know any longer. Maybe the connection she felt to him was all an illusion, brought on by sexual chemistry, an exhausting journey and the very slim possibility that they might well have a shared future neither of them had planned for. But she felt it nonetheless.

Whatever happened tomorrow, tonight, in this tent, in this desert, they were just two lonely people, and she wanted to know everything she could about him—and how he had become such a strong, indomitable ruler from such difficult beginnings.

His chest rose and fell in a heavy sigh as his fingers played with her hair. 'He didn't do it himself. He ordered his bodyguards to discipline me for trying to run away. But he always watched.'

Her fingers stilled on his chest. The chilling picture he painted dispelling the last of the afterglow.

'Zane?' She shifted so she could see his face, harsh and drawn in the half-light. 'I'm so sorry. That's horrific.' She imagined the violent marks that covered his back and buttocks and realised he must have been punished—or disciplined— like that more than once. What must it have been like for him? A boy torn away from everything and everyone he knew to live in a strange land, at the mercy of a man who was the opposite of a loving father?

'Don't be sorry,' he said, his thumb touching her cheek and trailing down to press against her pulse. 'It was a long time ago.'

'But even so, your own father... He was a monster.'

To her astonishment, Zane shook his head. 'He wasn't a monster. He was just a man who had been brought up to believe that everything he wanted should be his by divine right. And when he couldn't have the one thing he wanted the most, his mind became warped.' He sighed, the sound so hopeless it made Cat's heart hurt. 'Eventually I figured out it wasn't me he wanted to hurt,' he said, his voice hollow. 'It was her.'

'Your mother?' she asked, shocked by the casual revelation.

He nodded. 'He kept saying to me, over and over again, that she'd had no reason to leave him. Because he'd loved her more than life itself.' He huffed out a breath. 'I didn't get it back then— how toxic their love for each other was. All I knew was that he'd kidnapped me. And I hated him. So I kept running away, which was pretty damn dumb once I knew the consequences.'

She heard it then, the guilt in his voice— that made no sense at all. Cradling his cheek, she forced him to look at her. 'Of course you ran away. You wanted to go home. It certainly doesn't mean you deserved to be beaten.'

He covered her hand with his. 'So fierce,' he said, his lips tipping up in a wry smile.

Why was he looking at her like that? As if she'd said something cute?

'I don't understand why you're smiling,' she managed around the boulder of raw emotion in her throat.

'Do you really want to hear my life story?'

'Yes, I do, very much.'

He seemed surprised by her eagerness so she tried to dial it down. But it was hard with her heart pummelling her chest. Was he finally going to open up to her, at least a little bit?

'Why?' he asked.

Because I care about you.

She stopped herself from blurting out the truth. Whatever was happening between them, she didn't want to jeopardise it by revealing sentiments he might not return. Sentiments she wasn't even sure were real.

Was her fierce compassion for that boy just another by-product of the chemistry they shared?

'You never did give up on the idea of making me the centre of Narabia's story, did you?' he said, recalling the conversation they'd had three weeks ago.

Weeks that now felt like a lifetime. She wasn't sure she even cared about the project any more. Her desire to know more about that boy and what had shaped him wasn't about that any more, if it ever had been. But he had given her a way out. A means of getting him to talk about his past without her having to reveal how much she cared. And she couldn't stop herself from using it.

'I still think it's the most effective way to tell Narabia's story, yes,' she said.

'You really want the story to be that ugly,' he replied, but she could see he was considering what she'd said. And that in itself felt like progress.

'The truth is sometimes ugly,' she pointed out, even though it made her feel like a fraud. Wasn't she hiding the truth about how she was starting to feel about him?

Not about you, Cat.

'Whatever you tell me,' she continued, 'you would have an absolute veto on anything I put in the book. Obviously.'

And I would never put anything in there that might hurt you.

She knew she couldn't say that, even as she lay naked in his arms, her sex still pulsing from the intensity of his lovemaking.

But as he considered her words, she could feel a heavy weight pushing against her chest. The weight of responsibility and trust. Because they both knew, whatever did or didn't end up in the book, this would be a big step for him, he would be breaking a silence he'd held for a long time. For her. And that felt huge.

'All right,' he said at last. He wrapped an arm around her shoulders and tugged her gently off his chest, until she was snuggled against his side—and she couldn't see his face. Then he began to talk.

His voice sounded far away in the semi-darkness, the picture he painted of his childhood and adolescence so far removed from where they were now she could imagine it must have seemed to him as if he were describing someone else's life.

'I didn't run away when I got here because I wanted to go home so much. My mom wasn't a regular mom,' he began. 'She always liked to party too hard.' He shifted, his hand settling on her hair, but she bit back the questions already buzzing in her mind like hyperactive bees. She didn't want to interrupt. And discourage him.

'That only got worse as I got older. We moved out of the nice condo we had in the Hollywood Hills, and eventually ended up in a rundown apartment on Wilshire Boulevard. By the time I was fourteen, I would spend most nights dragging her out of some dive or other. She'd lost her looks, which meant even if she hadn't got a reputation for being difficult to work with, no one wanted to employ her any more. I had a job at a Korean grocery, but even working most nights after school, I couldn't keep up the rent payments.'

The uneasy flow of words cut off as he took several deep breaths; she could hear the guilt in his voice when he continued.

'I knew my old man was a big deal. A sheikh or a king or something. Because when she was really drunk she'd talk about him and Narabia, and the golden palace, about being a queen. How I was his heir and entitled to a fortune. And I'd checked out as much as I could about him online. I didn't believe all of it, it all seemed too freaky, but I figured even if he only had a bit of dough he could help us out. And by that summer I was desperate. We had tons of fights. I said all sorts of crazy stuff about how I hated her. How I'd be better off without her. I was fourteen and sick of the responsibility. I didn't want her weighing me down any more. We had a really big fight. I was so mad I poured every drop of liquor she had hidden round the apartment down the drain. She was crying and carrying on, telling me I was as much of a tyrant as my dad. I laughed in her face and said I'd rather live with a tyrant who had money than some broken-down nobody like her.'

Cat could feel the tension in his body, so she placed her hand on his heart, trying to ease the bitter memories. 'You don't have to continue.'

'Yeah,' he said. 'I do.' He paused, his hand covering hers, his thumb absently caressing the skin as he told her the rest.

'The next morning, she had the mother of all hangovers and a bad case of the DTs. But she was relatively sober for the first time in months, maybe years—she cried, she told me how sorry she was, for...' He paused, his body tensing. She could hear the deep draw of his breathing as his pain tightened like a vice around her own ribs. 'For messing everything up,' he said eventually. 'But I was still mad. So I left for school without even saying goodbye. My father's bodyguards snatched me off the street that afternoon and I never saw her again. She was dead two months later—an accidental overdose. My father showed me the newspaper article. And that's when I stopped trying to run away.'

He paused, the silence engulfing them both.

'Things got better after that, once I was willing to do what I was told. He wasn't what you'd call a loving father. But I've never had to worry about money again. So I figured I'd got what I wanted. My mom was the one who really suffered. Not me.'

She lifted her head. His blue eyes met hers, shadowed by shame and remorse.

Then he frowned. 'Hey, why are you crying?' he asked, touching the moisture on her cheek with his thumb. Moisture she hadn't even known was there.

She brushed the tear away with her fist, desperately trying to keep it together. Emotion pressed against her throat, making it hard for her to breathe, let alone speak.

'It's just such a sad story.' Although it wasn't a story, it was real. And it hurt her to think he still blamed himself for what had happened to his mother after he'd left. But she didn't know how to tell him that, without blowing her cover to smithereens.

'I told you it was ugly,' he said.

It wasn't ugly, she thought. It was desperately sad. Whatever had happened to pull his parents apart, to turn what had been a great love into a toxic relationship had left him caught in the middle—through no fault of his own. But she could see simply telling him that wasn't going to get through to him, because he'd lived with the shame and the guilt of his mother's death for a very long time.

'Would it be crossing a line if I told you something about myself, Zane?' she asked, hoping he would give her this opening, because for all her inexperience, and her naivety about relationships, there was one thing she did understand. What it was like to be a child, and blame yourself for something that had always been beyond your control.

The smile that tugged at his lips made him look so handsome. And so alone. 'You're naked in my bed, Catherine. I think we can say we've already crossed that line.'

She nodded, stupidly pleased by the humour in his voice.

'When I was six years old, my mother left my dad for another man. One of the many men she'd had affairs with. We never saw her again. And my father was devastated. It broke him in many ways.'

Zane's eyebrows rose up his forehead. Then he lifted his hand, and cupped her cheek. 'Hell, Catherine, I'm sorry. I didn't know that.'

She leaned into the gentle caress. 'It's okay. It was a long time ago now.'

'Yes, but... You were so young.'

And so were you, she wanted to shout at him. But she held back and began to talk instead, so he could understand he wasn't the only person who had made the mistake of thinking they were responsible for someone else's choices. That they could fix something—or someone—who had already been broken beyond repair.

'The thing is, Zane, I blamed myself. Because I'd told my dad about the man she was seeing. I didn't know it was an affair at the time. I just knew this guy was "Mummy's special friend", because that's what she called him when he came to the house when my father was at work. She told me not to tell my father. That it would be our secret. But I told him anyway. They had an enormous fight and then she left. And that's the last time I ever saw her.'

And ever since she'd blamed herself, not just for her mother's departure, but for her father's pain. Even if she'd never consciously admitted it to herself, the guilt had always been there. Why else would she have found it so hard to ever let herself be physically intimate with a man? Her attraction for Zane had been so overpowering she hadn't been able to deny it. But she could see now she'd always held herself back from sex because, in some childish, immature corner of her heart, she didn't want to be like her mother.

'That's about the dumbest thing I ever heard,' he said, cradling her face in his palms. 'You were six, Catherine. You couldn't have known what the hell was going on.'

She could smell soap on him and the scent of the sex they'd shared, and feel his heart pounding in strong steady beats beneath her cheek. He caressed her hair, cupping the back of her head—comforting her in the way she'd meant to comfort him.

She forced herself to draw away and look up into his face.

'I know. But I can see now for years I used what happened then as an excuse to be a coward in every area of my life.' *Until I made the decision to come to Narabia with you.* 'But if what happened with my mother wasn't my fault, how could what happened to your mother be your fault?'

'I'm not sure how the two are related,' he said, but he didn't look guilty any more, he just looked shattered. 'I was fourteen going on thirty with enough life experience to know better. You were just a little kid.'

His lips tilted in a devastating smile and his hand roamed up her thigh and squeezed her butt, sending delicious tendrils of heat skidding back into her sex.

It was a distraction technique, and they both knew it. But when he rolled over, and his erection brushed her hip, the shimmer of desire felt like a relief.

Who knew sex was by far the simplest and most straightforward part of any relationship to navigate?

'Are you trying to tell me something, Zane?' she asked with a soft laugh, deciding that simple was what they both needed now.

'No, I'm planning to show you,' he said. And then he kissed her, teasing butterfly kisses that sent her senses soaring, as he delved into her slick folds and found the swollen nub of her clitoris.

The soft laugh choked into a carnal moan of pleasure as she forgot about everything but the glorious feeling of being possessed by this powerful, complex man.

If this night was all they could have, it seemed foolish not to make the most of it.

'The Sheikh has left without me?' Cat stood in the soft morning light staring dumbly at the horizon, her heart beating an uneven tattoo.

Zane had brought her to climax twice more during the night. He'd taught her how to pleasure him using her hands, her mouth, her tongue… And had done the same for her, driving her to gasp and sob and cry out. But when one of Kasim's servants had woken her up half an hour ago, the tent had been empty, all traces of Zane gone—except the lingering scent of him that clung to her skin.

For a moment she'd even wondered if she'd dreamt the whole thing, the confidences they'd shared, the overwhelming emotions, the stunning intimacy.

When she'd finally tumbled into sleep she'd felt safe and secure in his arms. And now she felt bereft. She'd even been looking forward to the hour-long ride back to Allani, because it would give her one last chance to be with him, to be held by him.

'My brother left before dawn.' Kasim watched

her. And she was reminded of Zane's anger towards him the night before.

Kasim had arranged their night together to expose his brother to ridicule this morning. Was that why Zane had departed without a word? To save her reputation? It seemed the only explanation that made any sense.

She clung to it as she kept her face impassive. Or as impassive as she could while the vicious pain stabbed under her breastbone. She'd been abandoned once before. She could survive this, until she found out the reason why. And she was sure Zane had one.

'I see,' she murmured.

'He asked me to arrange a ride for you to Allani, where a vehicle will be waiting to drive you back to the palace,' Kasim said.

'But I don't know how to ride a horse,' she said, wondering why Zane hadn't mentioned she couldn't ride.

The sound of a loud snort startled her and she whipped around to see a group of men leading a line of camels. As the giant creatures drew closer, snorting and chewing and spitting, the pungent smell of urine and compost hung on the dry desert air.

'This is not a problem.' Kasim smiled, the easy grin reminding her of the far too charming man from the night before. 'Abdullah and his herders will show you how to ride a camel.' Leaning close to her, he whispered in her ear, 'But be sure to lean back on take-off and landing, or Zane will have my hide for compromising his woman's dignity.'

She found herself smiling back, the blockage in her throat making it impossible for her to correct him again.

Even if she could never acknowledge being Zane's woman, after everything they had shared last night she always would be in some small corner of her heart.

CHAPTER EIGHT

THE FOLLOWING WEEKS passed in a haze of hard work on the project, as Cat forced herself to forget about her brief liaison with the Sheikh.

She persuaded herself she'd overreacted about the things Zane had told her during their visit to the Kholadi camp and everything she thought they'd shared.

Because Zane was conspicuous by his absence.

When she'd arrived back from the Kholadi Oasis—after an eventful journey discovering the joys of camel riding—Ravi had greeted her to explain that His Divine Majesty would be unavailable for the next few weeks as he was travelling on a series of diplomatic missions to neighbouring kingdoms.

At that point she'd forced herself to bury her hurt and disappointment deep. Zane had made no promises to her, and she had made none to him in return. They'd simply been exploring their sexual connection. Nothing more or less. She needed to get her thoughts and feelings in perspective. In two months' time her visit to Narabia would be over and she would return to her life in Cambridge a wiser and more experienced woman. And if her nights were still filled with erotic dreams—that woke her up sweating and aching—that was a cross she would willingly bear for those two nights in Zane's arms.

And luckily, the work was exhilarating, with Ravi tasked to help and support her in everything she wanted to do. That Zane had lifted any embargo on her acting independently was a victory of sorts, which she tried not to read too much into.

With Kasia's assistance, she set up a series of group interviews with citizens across the spectrum of Narabian society. Before now, her work had always involved being a bystander, an observer, but with this project she felt so much more invested. And honoured to be even a small part of Zane's plans to bring Narabia's fascinating society into the glare of world attention.

Each evening when she returned to the palace she could hardly contain her enthusiasm about the conversations she'd had. And the progress she was making with the study. The only regret she had was that she couldn't discuss any of it with Zane. She would have loved to get his unique take on the country's complex culture and traditions.

She tugged her veil off, determined to keep the spurt of melancholy at bay as she and Kasia entered her chamber in the women's quarters.

The dusty road trip back from a small workers' encampment near the oil fields had been long and tiring—which was probably why she was dwelling on stuff that did not need to be dwelt on.

Zane and she weren't an item—they never had been. It had been a two-night fling.

'You look tired,' Kasia said as she poured water into the basin. 'We should cancel tomorrow's trip to Kavallah?' the girl added, now as good as fluent in English.

'I'm fine,' Cat replied, leaning over the basin to splash the cooling water on her face. The truth was she was exhausted, had been for several days, but that could only be because of the many sleepless nights she'd endured in the last few weeks.

She really needed to stop obsessing about Zane. And their mini fling.

'Ravi says the Sheikh has left today on a diplomatic mission to Zahar,' Kasia said as she filled another bowl with water and washed her own face.

Cat fought to quash the misery lodged in her chest, and the predictable colour climbing up her neck at the mention of Zane.

He was going about his business and she needed to do the same.

Eventually her appetite for him would fade—this was just a physical blip brought on by working too hard and not sleeping enough.

'When will you speak with him again, about the project?' Kasia asked as she lit the oil well beneath the Persian samovar Cat kept in her chambers—so they could have tea with the debriefing they always did after one of their field trips.

'I don't know,' she said, feeling stupidly dejected at the news Zane had gone off on another foreign trip without asking to see her.

'How long has it been that you and the Sheikh are together in his bed?' Kasia asked.

The hectic colour burned Cat's scalp. She

splashed more water on her face, trying and failing to cool the heat. The direct question was a surprise. Kasia and Ravi were the only people who knew she had spent the night with Zane in the palace all those weeks ago. She had been instructed never to mention it. And to Cat's surprise, she never had. Until now.

'Kasia,' Cat said, trying to speak calmly while the blush was running riot. 'You mustn't talk about that. I told you, it was a mistake.'

She had to believe that.

'I think maybe we must speak of it,' Kasia said, giving her a strange look.

A serving boy entered with a tray of the pastries they usually indulged in with their tea. The sweet confections made in layers of flaky patisserie and dripping with syrup were delicious, and Cat had become a bit addicted—but over the last couple of days she'd gone off them. And after today's long hot drive back, the rich treat definitely didn't appeal.

Filling a porcelain cup for Cat with the aromatic tea, Kasia handed it to her, then ladled a pastry onto a plate as the boy bowed and left.

'We definitely don't need to talk about it ever,'

Cat said, determined to steer the conversation back onto safer ground. She waved off the plate Kasia passed her way. 'I think I'll give the baklava a miss,' she said as the aroma of lavender syrup and pistachio wafted into her nostrils.

Her stomach turned over.

Kasia lowered the plate, but her face had brightened.

'It has been a month,' Kasia said. 'Since that night,' she continued. 'And now you cannot eat your baklava.'

'What?' Cat stared. It hadn't been a whole month, had it? She'd never counted the days, the prospect of a pregnancy so small. And her breasts had felt heavy, swollen recently, her stomach bloated, which had made her sure she was about to start her period.

Kasia nodded. Her smile radiant now. 'The Sheikh must marry you if you carry his heir,' she said, her voice giddy with excitement. 'And then you can stay in Narabia always as our Queen.'

Shock gripped Cat's insides—but with it came the emotion that had assailed her the night she'd drifted to sleep in the Kholadi camp, before Zane had arrived... The last time she had contemplated the possibility of pregnancy.

Before she could assess what the emotion was, exactly, her stomach heaved into her throat, bringing with it a wave of bile.

She dropped her tea, slammed a hand over her mouth. The sound of the porcelain chiming on the copper tray rang in her ears as she raced into the bathroom.

The contents of her stomach emptied into the toilet bowl in wretched spasms. Sweat misted her face, her limbs shaking as the retching continued until it felt as if everything she'd eaten that day had come out.

She slumped back on her haunches. A wet cloth covered her forehead as Kasia knelt beside her; her eager grin had a strange feeling of unreality settling over Cat.

But beneath that was a deep drawing need that was impossible to suppress.

'I can't be pregnant,' she said. Determined to believe it and ignore that strange wave of need— and something even more disturbing—making her hands shake.

A pregnancy would be a disaster, for her as well as Zane.

'I ate all that you ate, and I am not sick,' the girl replied. 'You are tired now these past days, and your breasts...' The girl's gaze dipped to the bodice of Cat's robe, which tightened around her torso like a titanium corset. 'They are more full, yes?'

'I can't be pregnant, Kasia,' Cat murmured again, starting to feel positively drained—the fear consuming her. She didn't want to cause a constitutional crisis, or force Zane into a marriage he didn't want. But what would happen if she were?

You're getting ahead of yourself, again. Nothing's confirmed.

'But you have not bled since you first lay with the Sheikh? Is this not so?' Kasia said, sounding perplexed at Cat's failure to be as overjoyed as she clearly was at the prospect of an unplanned pregnancy.

Cat dismissed the foolish clutch in her heart— and tried to control the terrifying emotion that had assailed her once before when she'd contemplated the possibility of carrying Zane's child.

'What's the actual date today?' she asked, her throat raw. She needed to get a grip. She wasn't always that regular. And she'd had a period only four days before her first night with Zane. And they hadn't used penetration during their night at the oasis. Surely there was no need to panic.

'The fifteenth of April,' Kasia said, starting to look concerned.

Cat frantically calculated the dates. Her heart jumped into her throat as she completed the maths.

Thirty-eight days since her last period.

She pressed a hand to her stomach. The panic and confusion accompanied by a deep jarring surge of protectiveness and that strange emotion she hadn't been able to name all those weeks ago at the oasis.

She sat down heavily on the divan. 'Oh, God,' she mumbled.

She'd never been this late before. Not even close. Against all the odds, she *could* be carrying the Sheikh's child. Zane's child.

Vulnerability opened like a huge chasm in the pit of her stomach.

'I think now the Sheikh will have to come back to the palace and speak with you,' Kasia said, her tone confident and amused at the prospect of that meeting.

The opposite of what Cat felt, because she now knew what that unnamed emotion was—however foolish and inappropriate in the circumstances—which had begun to choke her.

Not panic or shock or fear... But hope.

Your Divine Majesty,
Dr Smith has asked me to relay a request.
She asks if she can make an appointment to
speak with you on your return from Zahar
and wishes to know when that will be.
Regards,
Your humble servant,
Ravi

Zane stared at the note that had been passed to him by one of his advisors. The rambling welcome from the Crown Prince of Zahar in a dialect he didn't understand faded into the background as his gaze ran over the lines of the short missive again. And again. Emotions he'd struggled to tame over the last few weeks—during a series of increasingly desperate and interminably dull diplomatic missions—sprang up his torso. Alive and vivid and stronger than ever.

Passion. Desire. Concern. Surprise. But perhaps, most disturbing of all, a fierce sense of responsibility.

What possible reason could Catherine have for contacting him? Other than the obvious reason?

He'd been calculating the dates of their first encounter. And each day that had passed, his agitation had increased. He should have gone to see her, to confirm that she had had her period, long before now. But each time he had returned from another trip or tour, he had forced himself not to give in to the urge. Because he still hadn't managed to control the needs that raged through him every night.

It had nearly killed him to ease her out of his arms as the red light of dawn had shone through the fabric of the Kholadi tent nearly a month ago now. It had taken every ounce of his self-control to dress in the darkness and leave her succulent and responsive body lying naked on the sheets. To resist the intoxicating scent of sex twisting his guts into knots.

He'd done the right thing. He couldn't stay. Couldn't risk falling asleep in her arms. He'd already come perilously close to revealing the truth about what had happened the night before he'd been snatched by his father.

But in the weeks since he'd waited for the

need—and that terrifying sense of connection—
to fade.

Even though he hadn't told Catherine everything, he had told her things he had never con-
fided in anyone, an impulse that had made him
deeply uneasy the following morning.

But despite his desperation to create distance
between them in the weeks since… The need to
see her, to speak to her, to touch and taste her
hadn't died. If anything it had got worse. And
now this? He had not expected her to contact
him. Certain that she must realise absence was
the only way to curb their hunger for each other.

Even if it hadn't curbed it up to now.

He should ignore the note. He would be returning to the palace in two days. She hadn't
said the problem was urgent. Whatever it was.
And it would send entirely the wrong signals if
he rushed back to see her simply because she'd
asked him to.

But still the sense of urgency and anticipation tightened around his larynx, threatening to
strangle him as he remembered the silken soft-
ness of her hair against his fingertips, the brush
of her breasts shivering against his chest, as she
told him of the mother who had abandoned her.

He wasn't the only one who had made themselves vulnerable that night.

'Your Majesty, the Crown Prince would like to show you to his stables. He has a fine stallion to offer you as a gift.'

Zane's head rose at the whispered prompt from one of his diplomats.

So Prince Dalman had finally finished talking.

Crumpling up the note, he shoved it into the pocket of his robe. And before he could think better of it, he said what he had wanted to say as soon as he had read it.

'Tell the Prince I am very sorry, but I have urgent business and must return to Narabia.'

The advisor looked surprised, probably because he had transcribed the note and knew its contents, but he covered it well. 'Yes, Your Divine Majesty.'

The advisor made their excuses to Dalman, who looked suitably affronted at the abrupt change of plans.

As Zane left the palace and climbed into an SUV to take him to the nearby airfield, the obvious reason for Catherine's request occurred to him and a dropping sensation turned the need in his stomach into a hollow ache.

Of course, she had wanted to see him to tell him any chance of a pregnancy was now off the cards.

He rubbed a hand across his jaw, staring blindly at the jet as the airfield came into view and he recognised his reaction for what it was. Not relief, but disappointment. Bone-crushing disappointment.

'Damn it,' he cursed viciously under his breath. All the frustration and irritation of the last few weeks, which he had kept locked so carefully inside, finally coming out in the open.

What the heck was happening to him? This was madness. He didn't want Catherine to be pregnant. He didn't want her to have his child. Quite apart from anything else, if she became pregnant—and the news got out, which of course it would—he would have to force her to marry him. The way he suspected his father had once forced his mother.

History would repeat itself. Because how exactly was he supposed to explain to her that he would not be able to let her leave the country? That her free will would no longer be her own?

He didn't love Catherine, could never offer her

that, because he knew he could never allow himself to be that vulnerable again.

But even knowing that, a part of him—that dark, selfish part of him that had abandoned his mother without a backward glance—had hoped she would be pregnant. So he could make her stay. And the only possible reason for that was the hunger that had refused to die.

Need and desire reverberated through his body.

He imagined her kneeling in front of him, the way she had all those nights ago in Kasim's camp. Taking his swollen penis into her mouth, tentatively licking around the engorged head, her eyes dark with arousal and excitement as she concentrated on driving him to orgasm.

As he shifted in his seat, trying to relieve the pounding ache before he had to leave the car and get on the jet, he realised he had never been any better than the man who had hurt him. But even that wasn't enough to curtail the need.

'Ravi tells me you wished to see me.'

Cat tried to contain her nerves—and her shock at being summoned to Zane's office only three hours after she'd requested a meeting that morning. After her nausea attack yesterday, and another one this morning, she'd become more and more convinced she might actually be pregnant.

But she'd thought she would have several days to compose herself. To figure out what she wanted to do, before she would have to inform Zane of her symptoms. For that reason, and of course the need to keep her condition a secret, she had kept the note deliberately vague and non-committal.

The very last thing she had expected was to see him so soon.

The fact that the sight of him—magnificent in his ceremonial robes—had brought back memories of the last time she'd seen him, naked in her bed, wasn't helping with her composure.

'Thank you for agreeing to see me,' she said, not sure what the protocol was as the all-too-familiar flush crept up to her hairline.

His eyes narrowed and then his gaze darted to the door behind them. 'Ravi, leave us,' he said. 'I do not wish to be disturbed.'

If he thought the order odd, the chief advisor didn't say so, he merely bowed deeply and then left the room. Leaving them alone in the office.

Cat felt the intensity of Zane's gaze over every inch of her skin. Even in the ankle-length robe

she felt exposed, nervous, more than a little terrified of what his reaction would be when she revealed the reason she had asked to see him. She
took a deep breath, trying to gather the courage
she needed, when he spoke.

'Have you menstruated yet?' His gaze was
locked on hers, intense as always but also un-
readable. The nerves began to strangler her.

'No, I... I haven't,' she managed. 'I... That's
why I asked to see you.'

What was that tiny flicker of reaction on his
face? Surprise? Irritation? Concern? Why was
it so hard for her to tell what he was thinking?

He nodded, then indicated the deep leather
couch that stood under the office's arched windows. 'Sit down, Catherine, before you fall
down,' he said, his voice strained, but not un-
kind.

She perched on the seat, surprised when he
settled beside her and lifted her clutched hands
out of her lap. He ran his thumb over her knuckles; the spurt of longing shocked her so much she
tried to tug her hand back.

But he held on, then lifted his gaze. 'You have
been chewing your nails,' he observed. 'What
are you so nervous about?'

'I think…' She swallowed past the swell of emotion. What was he going to say and do? 'I think I may need to take a pregnancy test after all,' she finally got out.

He didn't drop her hand, as she had sort of expected. He didn't look angry or annoyed or even frustrated; his expression remained carefully neutral. But his fingers tightened reflexively on hers. The sure solid touch was somehow reassuring.

He seemed to absorb the news. Then he nodded. 'Have you had any other symptoms?' he asked, his tone surprisingly calm, she thought, seeing as her own throat felt as if it were burning.

'I've been sick a couple of times now, and my breasts have been swollen and oversensitive.'

His gaze dipped to her chest. 'Yes, I see your point.'

The flush fired across her collarbone.

He'd licked and suckled and played with her breasts that night at the oasis until he'd driven her wild with passion. So the idea she should be embarrassed by his observation now was absurd. But still it was a struggle to get the words out, while he sat next to her, exuding the raw sex appeal that had always captivated her.

'I thought I was about to start my period,' she said. 'But it's been thirty-eight days now. And I've never been that late before.' The babble of information finally stopped, the embarrassment crippling her, which was even more ludicrous.

His brows lowered fractionally, but it looked more like a frown of concentration than annoyance.

'How bad is the nausea?' he asked.

'Not too bad.' She huffed out a breath, finally managing to get up the strength to tug her fingers out of his. 'I'm so sorry, Zane. I know you didn't want this to happen.'

'Catherine, don't start apologising again.' He held up his hand. The wry smile boosting her confidence. At least he didn't seem to be angry. That had to be good, didn't it? 'First we will establish if there is a child.'

'Then what?' she forced herself to ask as he stood.

He captured her chin between his thumb and forefinger, and stroked the sensitive underside. 'Then we will consider the options open to us,' he said.

But as he let go of her face and strode to the door to get Ravi to call for the palace doctor to attend them, her heart ricocheted against her chest wall in hard, heavy thuds, like a bomb waiting to explode.

What options was he talking about?

'There is no mistake? Dr Smith is expecting a child?' Zane asked Dr Ahmed, the palace's physician, surprised he could keep his features controlled and his voice even, when all manner of thoughts and feelings were bursting in his chest.

Whatever happened now, Catherine was his responsibility. Catherine and his child.

'Yes, Your Divine Majesty. I estimate she is four weeks' gestation. The blood and urine tests both confirm this. And I can arrange for a sonogram tomorrow, at the clinic in Zahari,' he added, mentioning the nearest healthcare centre.

How ironic that one of his first actions as the acting Sheikh had been to invest in a network of state-of-the-art maternity clinics five years ago. He hadn't expected to need one himself quite so soon.

'Do it,' he said. He didn't want Catherine's care

compromised in any way. She was his woman now, no question.

'If this is how you wish to proceed?' the doctor said, his tone suggesting the remark was a question.

'Why wouldn't I?' he asked, confused by the man's reply.

'Can I ask, Your Divine Majesty, is the child yours?'

Zane had expected the medic to be curious; still it surprised him that the man was bold enough to ask the question. No one questioned the Sheikh. 'Yes, it is.'

The man's forehead creased in a thoughtful frown. 'This woman is not Narabian. Perhaps taking her to the Zahari clinic is not the best course of action—' the man cleared his throat '—as this will alert the populace to her condition—which would force Your Majesty's hand.'

Anger filled Zane, clutching at his stomach—what was this man suggesting? That he should not acknowledge the child as his? Or worse? But on the heels of it was the guilt that had crippled him as a boy.

This pregnancy was an accident. An accident they could have taken precautions to stop. But he'd wanted her to stay, so he'd been only too happy to let her take the risk. And now, if he acknowledged the child, she would be forced to marry him. Worse than that, she would effectively have no choice about continuing with the pregnancy.

But everything inside him rebelled against the idea of offering Catherine a choice. This was his child, his heir. He didn't want her to terminate the pregnancy. And he still wanted Catherine, more than he'd ever wanted any woman. Although this all-consuming desire would no doubt fade in time, it had been torturing him for over a month.

And from the breathless blush that had lit up Catherine's face when she'd mentioned her tender breasts, and his gaze had strayed to the provocative display of cleavage pressing against her robe, he knew it still tortured her too.

That the news of her pregnancy hadn't caused the panic he would have expected was perhaps a shock in itself. He had never even contemplated fatherhood until that first night with Catherine. But much more shocking was the realisation that however wrong, however selfish he was being, he didn't want to take the chance of losing her or his child.

Yet more proof that he wasn't as unlike his father as he had once assumed.

Letting the disgust rush up his throat, he sent the doctor a scathing glare.

'She will go to the Zahari clinic for her sonogram,' he said.

Realising his mistake, the doctor bowed profusely and babbled a series of apologies. Zane raised a hand to silence him. 'Arrange the appointment for tomorrow. I need to speak to Catherine in private.'

'Yes, Your Majesty,' the doctor said. 'She awaits you in my surgery.'

Opening the door into the doctor's surgery, he saw Catherine's head jerk up. She sat on an examination table, her robe replaced by a hospital gown. Unfortunately, the clinical outfit did nothing to disguise her voluptuous curves.

Arousal pounded back into his groin at the thought of his child nursing at those full breasts in eight months' time.

He wanted to see that, with a passion that surprised him. Apparently pregnancy was only going to make Catherine more irresistible.

Thank goodness they would have eight months to enjoy it before they would have to deal with the reality of a child.

But first he had to persuade Catherine that her future, their child's future, was here with him.

Maybe he couldn't offer either one of them love. But love was a fickle, dangerously destructive emotion—his own parents had taught him that.

What he could and would offer the child was his name and his heritage. And what he would offer Catherine was his protection, his wealth and, for as long as it lasted, every ounce of the passion now pounding through his veins.

'What did the doctor say?' Cat asked as Zane returned to the room. But she had already guessed when the palace doctor had left her, telling her he would have to inform the Sheikh first of her condition.

As a consequence, she'd been sitting on the clinic bed for the last twenty minutes trying to control the tangle of increasingly terrifying scenarios running through her head.

Capturing her hand, Zane sat beside her and slung an arm around her shoulders to pull her close to his side. His thumb ran across her knuckles, easing the trembling in her fingers. He nudged her hair with his chin, then placed a kiss on her cheek. 'It appears you are going to have my heir, Catherine.'

She let out a staggered breath, the panic releasing in a rush—washed away by the huge swell of emotion at his show of tenderness.

'You're not angry?' she said, unable to hold back the hiccup as tears stung her eyes.

'No. Are you?'

She shook her head, brushing a tear away with her fist. 'No, I'm...' What was she? Shocked? Overawed? Amazed? Joyful? Scared? All of those things and more. 'I'm not angry. It feels like a positive thing,' she added. 'Even if it's going to be challenging. What...? What will we do now?' she asked, feeling desperately unsure.

He'd said the baby would be his heir. But what did that mean? Would he ask her to stay in Narabia?

Giving up her life in Cambridge wouldn't be hard. She'd discovered an adventurous side to her nature in the last month and a half that would make it next to impossible to return to the cloistered, academic existence she'd lived there. Kasia was already a closer friend and confidante than any of the colleagues she had shared coffees and lunches and dinner and theatre dates with over the years. And as far as her academic studies went, she would relish the chance to spend years here, discovering all the secrets of this fascinating country.

But what would her life be like in Narabia as the mother of Zane's child? Would she be expected to live in the palace? How could she live here, so close to Zane, and not yearn to be with him? But what right did she have to ask for more? This was an accidental pregnancy and he'd already made it clear he had no desire to continue their brief sexual liaison. And even if he offered her more, how could she accept it, knowing that it was only being offered because she carried his child?

The thoughts rattled through her tired brain, starting to make her head hurt.

Taking her shoulders in firm hands, he nudged her round to face him, forcing her to meet the intense blue gaze that seemed able to see all of her weaknesses.

'So you want to have this child?' he asked.

She shuddered, his eyes stark with an emotion so intense it took her breath away.

She nodded, because at least the answer to that question was easy. 'Yes.'

He brushed his thumb across her cheek, gathering another tear. 'Then there's only one answer to your question. We will be married and you will become my Queen.'

'What?' His confident, pragmatic tone shocked her almost as much as the proposal.

His sensual lips tipped up into a smile that had her heart thundering against her ribs.

'You must marry me, Catherine,' he said again, as if it were the most obvious thing in the world.

Cat scrambled back, sure she must be dreaming now. Or in some strange fugue state brought on by the emotional overload of the last few days. 'But... I... I can't,' she said.

'Why can't you?'

'Because...' So many objections swirled in her head she couldn't cling to one. 'I'm not Narabian, for starters,' she managed. 'How could I possibly be your Queen? Surely your people would object to—'

'Shhh.' He touched a thumb to her lips, silencing the onslaught. 'I am half-American. My mother was American. The people embraced me and her because that was my father's choice. If I choose you, that is all the legitimacy we need.'

'But why *would* you choose me?' she murmured, the question striking at her greatest insecurity.

She'd watched her own parents' marriage disintegrate all those years ago, and she could still remember the words her father had spoken as her mother had left that night.

Please stay, Mary. Don't leave us. I love you. Cat needs you and we can work this out.

Her mother's reply still haunted her.

The problem is, Henry, I'm not sure I ever loved you. And I'm sure Cat will be fine without me. She's always been more loyal to you than me.

Her mother's departure had broken her father in so many ways. But it was those words—so flippant and callous and final—that had destroyed him. He'd been a good man, a dedicated father, but ever since that day something had gone out of him. He'd never smiled the way he had when her mother had been there, he'd never laughed with the same abandon.

On some level, Cat could see clearly now, she

had tried to fill the hole her mother had left behind, because she'd felt responsible for her departure—but she'd never been able to. Because she had lacked her mother's spirit, her mother's charisma, her mother's charm.

She couldn't bear to be cast in that role again. Even for the sake of her own child.

'Because you are going to have my child.' Zane's hand flattened against her belly. The warm possessive weight sent shivers throughout Cat's body. 'And because I still desire you, very much.'

'You do?' Cat blurted out. 'But I thought you didn't want me any more.'

'Why would you think that?' he said, his brows arching up his forehead.

'Because you left me at dawn. And you've avoided me ever since,' she said, admitting to herself for the first time how much his absence had hurt.

'I was trying to protect you,' he murmured.

'What from?' she asked, still confused.

'From me.' He huffed out a chuckle, the husky sound unbearably sexy. 'Which was pretty dumb in the circumstances.'

His gaze drifted down to where his hand now

caressed her belly in widening circles, making her sex throb in earnest.

His expression, dark with passion and intensity, made her belly float into her throat and her insides become giddy.

'I didn't know at the time I was shutting the stable door long after the damn horse had bolted and crossed the whole of the Narabian desert,' he added.

A laugh popped out of Cat's mouth, the unbearable tension dissolving as her heart lifted in her chest. She covered his hand with hers. 'I still desire you very much too,' she said. He still wanted her, as much as she wanted him. The realisation felt intoxicating. And powerful.

The amusement died on his face. Gripping her hips, he slid her across the bed, and lifted her into his lap. She grasped his shoulders, her knees straddling his hips as the gown rose up. She felt the muscles bunch and tighten beneath her hands, his breath gushing out as his hands rose up her back, drawing her towards those sensual lips that had always promised so much and delivered even more. The ridge of his erection butted against her sex, and she rubbed her yearning clitoris against it. His lips captured hers.

The kiss was urgent, demanding, possessive, his tongue sweeping inside her mouth, and claiming her in the most elemental way possible. She ground against his length, the contact too much and yet not nearly enough.

Her fingers threaded into his hair, clasping, clinging, dragging him closer.

The feeling of connection, of empathy, of need blossomed inside her. This passion, this desire, had to mean something, didn't it?

The insecurities that had battered her burned away as he devoured her mouth.

He dragged her head back at last. 'Damn it, we can't. Not here. Not now,' he said, his tone rough with frustration.

He lifted her off his lap and stood up. The thick erection was still prominent in his suit pants. 'We should wait,' he said. 'Until after the wedding.'

'The wedding?' she said, still dazed and yearning.

Then to her astonishment he sank to his knees in front of her. The gesture was so romantic, her heart stopped.

He gripped her hands in his much larger ones, quelling the shaking as all the insecurities his kiss had swept aside came rushing back.

'Marry me, Catherine, and become my Queen,' he said, his voice so full of purpose she felt her heart dissolve.

She should say no, a voice whispered in her head. This was a proposal born out of duty and passion. And how could that ever be enough? They hadn't even discussed an emotional commitment. He didn't love her. And she already knew it would be far too easy for her to fall hopelessly in love with him.

But all the questions, the doubts, hung on her tongue as the spontaneous bubble of hope expanded in her chest.

Marriage was a big step, but having a baby together was a huge one. And that was a step they were already taking.

This wasn't an end, it was a beginning. And surely duty and passion were something sturdy they could build on while they got to know each other better. In every way.

The blush rose up her throat at the thought of how much pleasure they could have discovering just some of those ways.

And even love didn't come with guarantees, she reasoned frantically. It could be reckless and fickle—the way it had been for her mother. Or become twisted and destructive—as it had been for Zane's parents.

Surely this was a chance to learn from those mistakes? And start out right? Why couldn't this marriage lead to something wonderful? He wanted her, and he was a good man. Not just gorgeous and ridiculously sexy, but also strong and responsible and so protective.

And he was the father of her child.

Zane rubbed the backs of her hands with his thumbs. 'My ego is dying here, Catherine,' he said in a hoarse, self-deprecating chuckle.

But she heard the slight edge in his tone—proving he was more concerned about her answer than he was letting on—and that tiny glimmer of insecurity was enough to allow the hope to expand and push aside the doubts.

'Okay,' she said, suddenly shy when the tension in his jaw released and an assured smile spread across his features.

'Thank God,' he said. 'I'm not used to spending so long on my knees,' he added and they both laughed.

Standing, he tugged her off the bed, until she was flush against the line of his body, his arms banded around her.

Happiness filled her as he stroked her back.

She mattered to him. They both wanted this. And that was more than good enough for now.

'The wedding will need to be a state occasion,' he murmured against her hair. 'But I'll instruct Ravi to keep it as small and manageable as possible. I've waited more than long enough already to have my woman in my bed again.'

The urgency and possessiveness in his tone was like an aphrodisiac. He clasped her face and pressed a kiss to her forehead, and the deep well of yearning opened inside her.

But then the same feeling of vertigo that had crippled her when he'd first persuaded her to come to Narabia paralysed her again. Because this time the cliff was so much higher, the landing so much more uncertain and her ability to stop herself from tumbling over the edge so much more unsure.

CHAPTER NINE

THE SMALL AND manageable ceremony Zane had alluded to on the day of their engagement turned out to be anything but.

After a week of planning and preparation, a five-day tour of Narabia was arranged—during which Catherine was introduced to her new subjects as His Divine Majesty's betrothed. Once they had returned to the palace, two days of feasting with five hundred invited guests were followed by a lavish ceremony in which Cat signed a lengthy document and then Zane made a series of solemn vows to support Cat and their children before presenting her with a gold chest full of jewels that looked to her like a prop from a Hollywood pirate movie.

The whole experience was overwhelming; as the marriage ceremony finally began to draw to a close, Cat felt as if she had stepped into an alternative reality.

Other than the series of fittings with a team

of dressmakers to make her a wardrobe fit for a queen, the endless meetings with Zane's financial, legal and religious advisors to brief her on the customs and legalities of the marriage, and the intensive language lessons she'd embarked upon with Kasia to learn enough so she could converse fluently with her new subjects during the betrothal tour, Cat had had no part in the organisation.

She didn't mind. She already felt overwhelmed enough by the prospect of marriage to such a powerful, intoxicating man and the realities of her pregnancy—which made themselves felt quite forcefully each afternoon.

In fact, she was glad she hadn't had to do much during the ceremony itself. The feasting had been exhausting enough with her and Zane situated on two gilded thrones while the neighbouring princes, kings and dignitaries came to pay their respects to the Sheikh's new bride. She tried to learn all their names and answer them as best she could in the Narabian language. She was pathetically grateful to see a familiar face when Kasim marched into the hall in full battle dress, flanked by an honour guard of his tribesman. After giving a sweeping bow before Zane and her, he winked at her and for the first time in days she found herself smiling—when he whispered, 'So it seems you are Zane's woman after all?'

She hid a laugh behind her hand. The man was incorrigible, his dark eyes tempting her to share the joke.

'You must name your firstborn after me,' he added for her ears alone. 'As I believe the babe was conceived in my camp.'

She blushed, making Kasim laugh.

She shifted her gaze to Zane, who was watching them both intently, and hoped no one else had heard Kasim's claim.

The pregnancy was not yet common knowledge—even though Zane's advisors had assured her there would be no need to hide the fact the baby had been conceived before the nuptials.

Marriage in this culture was about practicalities, they had told her. A union between two like-minded souls in which the man was required to prove he would always protect and nurture his wife and their children.

She assumed it was the weight of that responsibility, as well as the many legal and constitutional practicalities Zane had to observe in the run up to the marriage, that explained why she had barely seen him during the past two weeks. And when she had seen him, she'd detected a strange distance, as if he were constantly distracted.

He'd done his very best to prepare her for the responsibilities that would fall to her as his Queen. But even so she felt exhausted when she and Kasia finally left the festivities and made their way to the bridal chamber.

She stood on the balcony in the elegant chamber, which the palace staff had spent days preparing for her, and watched the pop and sparkle of fireworks light up the night sky above the courtyard.

Kasia set about filling a copper tub with steaming water, while Cat listened to the music and merriment from the wedding celebrations, which were still in full swing.

Goosebumps rose on her arms and she rubbed the sensitive skin as Kasia helped her out of the scarlet robe, edged with gold thread, which she had worn during the ceremony.

She'd felt Zane's eyes on her all day, and now her skin felt too tight, her breasts tender and swollen, her belly alive with the tangle of anticipation and anxiety that had dogged her for days as they'd both conducted what had seemed like a never-ending roster of official duties.

She still wasn't entirely sure what she'd got herself into. But what had felt like a marvellous adventure after his proposal didn't feel quite so uncomplicated any more.

She already knew she was in love with this diverse, fascinating country and culture, and its people.

But much more disturbing were her feelings for Zane.

She was already more than halfway in love with this man. But in the past two weeks, as she'd been prepared for the marriage, paraded around the kingdom by his side without ever getting a chance to talk to him properly and then serenaded and feted during the feasting and the final ceremony, she had begun to realise how little she knew him.

They were virtual strangers. That night in the tent, when he had shared a few tragic details of his childhood, seemed so long ago now. The glimpse she'd got of that vulnerable and lonely LA teenager a million miles away from the in-

domitable, autocratic ruler whom she had become so aware of in the last few days.

Kasia helped her into the large copper tub.
Cat let out a deep sigh, sinking into the heated
water—and tried to force herself to relax—as
the scent of lavender filled her nostrils.

'You are truly the most beautiful bride,' Kasia
said dreamily, working to unpick a hairdo that an
army of stylists had taken several hours to create that morning. 'The Sheikh did not take his
eyes from you the whole day. He is a man very
much in love, I think.'

Cat's heart clutched painfully at Kasia's romantic statement.

'Zane's chief cultural advisors told me love is
not a requirement of a successful Narabian marriage, especially for the Sheikh,' she said.

She had tried not to overreact at their insis-
tence on mentioning this pertinent fact over and
over again during her briefings. She had tried to
convince herself the repeated warnings about
the fickle, mercurial nature of such emotions
was simply a necessary part of their job to inform her of Narabia's culture and customs. Or
maybe they were just being overcautious, trying
to assess if she would be as much of a liability

as Zelda Mayhew, after the love match between Zane's parents had ended so disastrously.

But after being told this 'fact' several times, she had begun to wonder if this warning was coming from Zane, instead of his advisors. Had he briefed them on what to say to her?

Of course, it would be foolish of her to get upset about it even if he had. She'd agreed to this marriage knowing full well they hadn't declared any deeper feelings for each other... But even so it had made her feel increasingly insecure.

Had she made a terrible mistake agreeing to this marriage? What if Zane didn't believe in love? Or, more importantly, what if he wasn't capable of loving her? After spending two weeks involved in all the pomp and circumstance surrounding their wedding, she certainly couldn't underestimate any more how big a step it was to agree to marry the Sheikh.

But why did she suddenly feel so vulnerable? What had happened to that balloon of hope that had made her say yes in the first place?

'Pfft!' Kasia scoffed, as she massaged shampoo into Cat's scalp. 'What do a load of old men know about love anyway?'

Cat pushed out a laugh at Kasia's irreverence,

trying to ignore the apprehension that had been building for days now, but the breathless chuckle sounded strained even to her.

'The Sheikh is so handsome and he wants only you,' Kasia insisted as she rinsed Cat's hair—the luxurious pampering helped relieve the tension tying the muscles of her neck into tight knots. 'Tonight he will make you his again. And then you will know how he feels.'

Cat doubted she would know that much. But at least she would feel much more secure. It was Zane's distance in the last fourteen days that had allowed all her insecurities to flourish.

Once she was back in Zane's arms the hope and euphoria would return. She was exhausted and on edge, never a good combination for a pregnant lady.

Of course, she didn't know Zane yet. They'd slept together twice and been married for approximately two hours. And they had only managed to share three private conversations since he'd proposed. All three of which had consisted of him asking her if she was nauseous, if the marriage arrangements were too stressful and if she was getting enough sleep.

He'd been kind and considerate, attentive and

solicitous—despite the enormity of the responsibilities weighing him down. She was blowing everything entirely out of proportion. Kasia was right, tonight was the beginning of a new phase in their relationship. A stunning new adventure.

Maybe they had never spoken about love. But they had spoken about commitment. Because what could be more of a commitment than marriage?

He'd made her his Queen, for goodness' sake, and here she was freaking out over something— a shared intimacy—that could only develop over time.

She forced herself to sink into the water—and put all the what ifs out of her mind—as Kasia finished washing her hair.

The bridal chamber was lavishly furnished and had a walk-in wardrobe full of the clothes the dressmakers had made for her over the last two weeks.

She and Kasia spent half an hour selecting the perfect night robe for her marriage bed. They sipped the spicy fruit liquor that had been left in the chamber to help relax her as Cat tried on the different outfits.

It reminded her of her first night with Zane.

The night she and Kasia had snuck into his mother's salon. Who would have thought only six weeks later she would be waiting to spend her wedding night with this remarkable man?

Anticipation turned to desire as she stared at herself in the mirror. The robe they had eventually chosen was in a deep purple and although not as elaborate as her wedding robe, it was a great deal more revealing. Especially as Kasia had been adamant she mustn't wear any lingerie.

'The Sheikh will not want to wait. And neither will you,' she had said, as if she were an experienced courtesan instead of a nineteen-year-old virgin.

The shadow of Cat's nipples, already enlarged in pregnancy, and the hair covering her sex, which had been trimmed by the beautician that morning, were clearly visible through the shimmer of silk.

Gold and silver thread and what looked like real gemstones were embroidered in Moorish patterns in the robe's bodice and hem. The garment flowed around her, accentuating her curves, while the deep V almost reached to her navel.

Kasia had spent ages brushing and drying her hair after her bath. The thick waves sparkled in the candlelight, while a few curls had been teased out to caress her cheeks.

Kasia had also washed off the heavy wedding make-up and replaced it with the barest hint of lip gloss, which made her mouth glisten in the evening light.

Cat sucked in a tortured, tremulous breath.

Her skin hummed with agonising sensation, as if she were being stroked all over at once.

Kasia grinned at her in the mirror, her face a picture of approval and anticipation.

She didn't recognise herself as the mousy academic who had first met Zane less than three months ago in Walmsley's office. She looked sultry and sexy and bold, in charge of her own sexuality. Which wasn't entirely true. She still wasn't the most experienced woman on the planet.

But over the next weeks and months that would change.

Getting to know Zane—getting close to him, learning what made him tick, discovering his likes and dislikes, his strengths and weakness— was going to be an adventure equally as exciting and exhilarating as becoming Narabia's Queen and unlocking the limits of the passion they shared for one another. And then they would be embarking on a whole new adventure when their baby was born.

She'd already begun to sample the good stuff. This dramatic change in her life and circumstances was overwhelming at times, but that was only because it was so unexpected. Nothing had prepared her for this journey, but that didn't mean she couldn't adapt and enjoy it.

All she needed to do was embrace each new experience as it came and not panic herself into an early grave, before she got to the best stuff.

Love had gone terribly wrong, for both her parents and Zane's; neither of them had any experience of a happy marriage. But perhaps that was a good thing. It would make them more cautious, more measured. Maybe Zane's advisors were right after all.

Love would be so much stronger if it grew out of shared intimacy, shared responsibility, rather than some ephemeral notion based on nothing more than an incendiary physical attraction.

'Leave us, Kasia.'

Cat jerked round to see Zane's large frame filling the arched doorway of the chamber.

He no longer wore the full ceremonial robes he'd donned for the marriage ceremony. The sabres, his boots and headdress were gone. His closely cropped hair shone black in the glimmer of candlelight. But he still looked magnificent, the loosely fitted dark trousers covered by an embroidered tunic, which had an open V down the middle, revealing far too much of that impressive chest.

A new bolt of heat loosened Cat's already trembling thigh muscles.

'Yes, Your Divine Majesty.' Kasia bowed deeply, then fled from the chamber, but not before sending Cat a mischievous grin, which reminded her of the grin her friend had sent her once before. The first night she'd slept with Zane.

Not just Zane any more. Her new husband.

She pushed a staggered breath out of tight lungs as he walked towards her, his bare feet muffled on the thick silk rugs.

'You look exquisite,' he murmured as he brushed his thumb against the pulse that was battering her collarbone.

'Thank you,' she said. 'So do you.'

He laughed, the deep chuckle disconcerting. She hadn't meant to say anything amusing.

'I thought that damn ceremony would never end,' he added. His thumb drifted down to circle the nipple poking against the transparent silk of her robe.

It tightened painfully, and she gasped. Shocked by the instant arousal, the flood of moisture even his slightest touch could evoke.

Passion erupted at her core.

'Are they more sensitive?' he asked, and she nodded.

Why did her live-wire reactions to this man suddenly feel too extreme, too needy?

'This is a beautiful robe,' he said, stroking the thin silk, but then he curled his fingers around the lapels and tore it away from her body. 'But entirely superfluous.'

The sound of rending fabric filled the chamber, and she jerked in shock. But then her gaze connected with his and she saw the brutal passion, the desperate demand. And desire exploded inside her, sweeping everything before it—doubts, fears, insecurities—until all that was left was the all-consuming need.

The torn silk whispered over her skin and pooled around her ankles, leaving her stunned and yearning in front of him.

The desire to cover herself whispered across her mind, but before she managed to gather herself enough to act upon it he bent and lifted her into his arms.

He carried her into the next room. A large bed stood in the middle of the chamber, the frame decorated with garlands of flowers. The heady perfume seemed to engulf her, but as he laid her down on the soft sheets and she watched him tear off his own clothes nothing in her mind seemed to register except the sight of him.

All that power, all that passion, was concentrated in the hard lines of his body, the smooth dark skin, the bulge and flex of sinew and muscles, the ragged scars on his back, the powerful jut of his erection.

He climbed onto the bed and rubbed the heel of his palm against her yearning clitoris. She bucked off the bed. And he traced the slick folds with his fingers, while leaning over her to capture one rigid nipple in his mouth. He suckled hard on the sensitive peak, making her cry out, drawing the brutal orgasm forth as he found the tight nub with his thumb.

She sobbed, moaned, trying to hold on, trying to hold back. But she felt trapped by her own desires, driven wild by a need that stunned her.

As she crashed over that final edge, sensation

fired through her body like the fireworks she had witnessed earlier. Bright colourful lights, stunning and surreal, rippled through her nerve endings. Before she had a chance to regroup, to recover, he moved to grasp her hips, angle her for his possession, and the huge head of his erection pressed into the swollen folds.

He felt immense, impaling her too-sensitive flesh, the wide girth stretching her, filling her.

She clung to his shoulders, the brutal orgasm not allowed to ebb as he set a punishing rhythm. Thrusting deep, then drawing back.

The orgasm crested again, hurling her back into the maelstrom as he butted a spot deep inside her.

'Come for me again, Catherine.' His voice, deep and tortured, demanded and she delivered.

He grew even bigger inside her as she sobbed her surrender.

He grunted, harsh and long. The moan echoed around the chamber as his seed emptied into her.

In the afterglow-infused haze, her body struggled to adjust. He withdrew swiftly and moved off her. Then pulled the sheet up over her shaking body.

Leaning over her, he pressed his lips to her

forehead, as he had done the afternoon of the proposal. But this time the kiss felt perfunctory. Especially when he rolled away from her and stood. He began to walk towards the balcony that connected their two suites of rooms.

'Zane, where are you going?' she said, the brutal urgency of his lovemaking still echoing between her thighs, still making her breasts prickle and pulse.

She saw his back stiffen, the ragged scars standing out against the smooth skin, the flicker of candlelight making them seem even more grotesque. Even more tragic.

'I'm returning to my own chamber,' he said, his voice dull and flat and devoid of the warmth she had come to expect.

She scrambled up in bed, clinging to the sheet, desperate to cover her nakedness, feeling more exposed than she had when he'd ripped away her robe. 'But aren't you going to sleep here… with me?'

He turned back, and those sensual lips lifted in a smile that didn't reach his eyes.

Even naked, he looked every inch the Sheikh in that moment and nothing like the man she thought she had agreed to marry.

'I have my own suite of rooms on the other side of the courtyard, Catherine. I prefer to sleep alone.'

'You... You don't want to be with me,' she said, her voice thick with tears. What was wrong? Why was he treating her like this? He seemed more distant now than ever.

Placing a knee on the bed, he cupped her cheek; she leaned into it, the sign of warmth, of tenderness the first one he'd shown her since entering the room.

'Don't get upset, Catherine,' he said. 'We'll make this work.' His gaze dipped to her abdomen as he stroked her cheek. 'For you and me, and the baby.'

Her breath shuddered out. Thank God, he understood.

But then his eyes seemed to flatten, the light going out of them. And he drew his hand away. 'But I'm afraid there's no room for sentiment in this marriage.'

Sentiment? What did that even mean? Was he talking about intimacy?

But before she could get the questions tumbling around in her tired, overwrought mind out of her mouth, he added, 'I told my advisors to make that abundantly clear. I thought you understood.'

The horrifying statement had all the things she'd feared, all the things she'd assumed were paranoid delusions, turning to stark, cruel reality.

He strode away through the arched doorway and out onto the balcony, gloriously naked, his taut body limed by moonlight. As the soft pad of his footsteps disappeared, a sob lodged in her throat.

For goodness' sake, get a grip.

She shoved the panic down.

He's new to this too. We can work this out. He just needs to get used to me.

But still the tears coursed down her cheeks.

Because even as she reasoned he was only a few rooms away, it felt as if a thousand miles separated them now.

Zane stood under the shower, letting the hot spray ease the wretched regret making his throat ache. But it couldn't do anything for the despair.

This marriage was going to be so much harder than he had anticipated. Keeping his emotions, the foolish rush of need in check—for more than just sex—was going to be torturous. He'd realised it as soon as he'd walked into the bridal chamber and seen Catherine, her expression so open, so hopeful.

The arousal had been swift and sure as it always was with her. But on the heels of it was the knowledge he could never be what she needed.

He'd spent the last two weeks trying to establish the distance he needed to make this marriage work, by filling the hours with duties and responsibilities and ensuring his advisors explained to her the parameters of their relationship. But in the space of a few hours, as she'd sat next to him on the podium while the wedding festivities had raged around them, he'd known his feelings weren't as circumspect as they needed to be. Not when she looked at him like that, with so much tenderness in her eyes.

From now on he would have to manage the hunger, and find a way to control the intimacy. He couldn't let her get any closer, or she would discover the man he truly was inside.

Not a ruler, not a king, not a sheikh, but a scared, lonely boy who had betrayed his own mother to save his own skin.

CHAPTER TEN

Three months later

ZANE WALKED INTO his private quarters with his secretary hovering at his heels. 'Cancel the Umara mission. I've had enough conversations about fertiliser to last me the rest of the month.'

He ripped off his headdress and handed it to the manservant who was waiting in his dressing chamber.

Three days and nights. Three days and nights he'd been without her and he felt as if he were about to burst out of his own skin. When the hell was this hunger for her going to end?

The thought had tortured him for the last three days as he'd sat through endless diplomatic meetings with Prince Alkardi. While he'd listened to interminable garbage about trading treaties and farming rotations with a placid smile on his face while all he'd been able to see or think about was Catherine—her cheeks flushed with passion, her eyes bright with amusement during a state visit they'd done to a local school the day before he'd left. Or that tempting wrinkle of concentration between her brows when she'd spoken to him last week about her idea to set up a women's congress.

Three months they had been married and he still hadn't found the distance he needed to make this marriage work.

Shooing the secretary away, he marched into the bathing chamber as he pulled his tunic over his head.

'Where's the Queen?' he asked as the manservant gathered the tunic. Why wasn't she here, waiting for him? He had assumed she would be here. Hadn't he sent word ahead that he had decided to cut his mission short a day early? He felt the prickle of temper at her absence. He'd had plans for this evening, which was why he had raced home. Plans that did not involve soaking in the fragrant pool of steaming water his manservant had prepared for them both all on his own.

'The Queen is on a visit today to the marketplace to publicise the new congress, Your Majesty,' the young man said, dropping to one knee.

'Send word that I wish to see her,' he snapped,

then regretted the curt, ill-tempered reply when the young man flinched.

When had he become as impatient and autocratic as his father?

Thoughts of his father had a new spike of temper festering in the pit of his stomach. He wasn't a tyrant. He respected women. He respected Catherine, more than he could say, but he had been without her for three days.

Amir jerked up, poised to dart out of the room.

'And, Amir, there is no need for you to return. Take the rest of the day off. I wish to see the Queen in private.'

Amir hesitated. 'You do not need me to help you undress and bathe, Your Excellency?'

'No, I do not,' he said. Because he intended to ask Catherine to take over that task. The knot in his gut loosened a little as Amir executed a deep bow, then sped out of the room.

He thrust his fingers through his hair as he walked into the adjoining washroom to the pool chamber. For once he didn't care if he sounded like a tyrant. A little urgency wouldn't do Catherine any harm at all.

He'd treated her well these past three months. He hadn't made too many demands. He'd supported her in her role as Queen and been considerate of her pregnancy. He had limited himself to coming to her chambers every other night... Thank goodness she had finally stopped requesting he stay with her after they had satisfied the physical urge that would not die.

But tonight he felt irritable. As if something was bubbling under his skin that had been bubbling for a while. The trip had exacerbated the feeling, had definitely made it more acute, but that feeling had been there for weeks now.

He sat on the divan and yanked off his boots, then stood to untie the sash around his waist. He kicked off his pants, but as he whipped open the cabinet above the marble vanity to find his razor, he spotted the bottle of pregnancy vitamins she kept there.

He touched the small bottle with his fingertip and realised that it was nearly empty. The dropping sensation in his stomach twisted in his abdomen. And he cursed under his breath.

He'd tried not to notice the way her body had changed in the last few months. The nausea had stopped over a month ago, but her breasts had only become more tender, more sensitive, her body more voluptuous as it ripened in pregnancy.

He rubbed a hand across his jaw, staring blindly at the bottle. And finally forced himself to acknowledge what had been bothering him for the last few weeks.

The baby. And the fact that it would be impossible to avoid discussing it much longer.

Catherine was already four months pregnant. Eventually, he would have to stop coming to her bed.

He braced his hands on the marble unit. Need and desire reverberated through his body.

He reached down to grasp the base of the painful erection. Closing his eyes, he pumped his fist up and down, feeling the tug on his skin, trying to picture her there, doing it for him.

He cursed violently and let go, because the image wasn't enough. He slapped his palms down on the marble. Sickened by his own desperation. The feral need rioting through his veins that only she seemed capable of satisfying.

This was becoming an obsession. He needed to stop this now. To control this yearning, these urges. It had been a mistake to bring her so closely into his life. To indulge himself to this extent. By doing so he had unleashed a beast. The same beast he had always known was there, and now he was very much afraid he might never be able to control it again.

He stared at his face in the mirror. And saw the harsh planes and angles of his father's face. A face that had once haunted him in nightmares. Tension screamed across his shoulder blades, made his buttocks flinch as the skin burned and pulsed with the phantom pain of the whip.

The erection mercifully began to wilt.

He was having some kind of weird emotional crisis, that was all, brought on by stress and the enforced celibacy of the last three days. This was about sex. Watching Catherine's body blossom and her confidence grow as his Queen had been captivating and fascinating and wildly erotic. But once she had the child, once they stopped sleeping together—or rather having sex together— he would be able to return to who he had been before.

Perhaps he should call a halt now. Make a clean break. Waiting any longer would only make the need worse. He would miss the spectacular sex with a woman he had an undeniable chemistry with. But his inability to be without her for a scant three days proved he had become fixated on her. His emotions had become too close to the surface. He had to re-establish the control that had been so hard-earned when he had first arrived in Narabia.

Taking a drying cloth off the neatly stacked pile Amir had left for him, he wrapped it around his nakedness.

'Zane?' Catherine's voice, urgent and familiar, coming from her own chamber, echoed in his chest. 'Where are you?'

'Here.' His voice sounded gruff, not his own as he marched into the pool room to greet her.

She rushed towards him and threw her arms around his waist. 'Zane, you're back a day early,' she said, bright and eager. Why did it feel so good to know she had missed him too?

He should pull away, but he couldn't seem to stop himself wrapping his arms around her shoulders and drawing her flush against his body.

The blood charged back into his groin as he dropped his cheek to the unruly wisps of hair and drew the scent of her shampoo—chamomile and honey—deep into his lungs.

'Where have you been?' he said, more harshly than he had intended as the desire tormented him.

She dropped her head back, tilted her chin up to look into his eyes—and for a moment he saw something flicker there, something wary and unguarded.

But before he could decipher it, her face stretched back into that bright smile. 'Kasia and I only just got back from—'

For once he didn't care, cutting off the explanation as he scooped her up and she yelped, grasping his shoulders.

'Zane!'

'I hope you're not wearing panties,' he demanded, trying to sound playful and amused when all he felt was wild—as the grinding need he hadn't been able to control pounded back into every pulse point.

She gripped his shoulders, her surprised chuckle like a whip to his senses as he marched into the pool with her in his arms.

Within minutes he had wrestled her out of her wet clothes and discarded his. He pressed her back against the mosaic tiles, ripped the offending panties off and then lifted her into his arms to impale her on the thick erection.

She sobbed, her breasts bobbing in the water,

her face glowing with sweat and steam as he drove inside her to the hilt.

But as he thrust out and back, forcing her towards orgasm, letting the madness, the need overtake him, spurred on by her jagged sobs, frantic to reach that final peak, the terrifying thought kept pushing at the back of his mind that no matter how many times he did this—no matter how many times he watched her shatter around him, felt her massage his length in the throes of her release—it would never be enough.

And no matter how many times he told himself he didn't need her, he might never, ever be ready to let her go.

'Zane, is everything all right?' Cat asked as she clutched his shoulders, the water beginning to cool around them.

'It was a long boring trip,' he murmured against her hair before lifting her out of the water and placing her on her feet.

Her heart shrank in her chest, as it did every time he avoided talking about his feelings. She thought they'd made progress in the last few months. Had forced herself to be optimistic about their marriage. And when his manservant had come rushing into the women's quarters to tell her, not only that he had returned early from his three-day trip, but that he wanted to see her immediately, and in private, her spirits had soared.

This had to mean something.

He'd taken her with passion and as always she'd revelled in it. But for the first time afterwards, the optimism she'd tried to feel each night he'd left her bed refused to come.

He handed her a towel and bent to pick one up himself. She knew she was about to be dismissed. And for the first time ever, instead of trying to fill her head with positive thoughts, with patience and compassion at the sight of his scars, she felt the first stirrings of anger.

She'd waited for him to meet her halfway, to finally admit that there was more in this marriage than duty and sex, but it had been three months now. And he still refused to meet her even a quarter of the way.

Just as she was about to say something though, she felt a strange tickling sensation in her abdomen. She gasped and pressed her hand to her belly.

Zane shot round, his eyes concerned. 'What's the matter? Are you okay?'

'Yes, I…' She gasped again as the tickling sensation rippled across her palm.

'What is it, Catherine? Is something wrong?' He gripped her arms, his face a mask of shock and pain and guilt.

But she didn't have time to ask herself where that look was coming from before the smile split her face in two.

'What…?' He stepped back, letting her go.

'It's okay.' Lifting his palm on impulse, she flattened it over her belly. 'It's Junior. I think we woke him up.'

She laughed, the sound echoing around the steamy chamber, her joy uncontrollable. They had a child. A baby. Which would make everything right. She'd been telling herself as much for months. Convincing herself that Zane would come around. But instead of the interest, the fascination, the matching joy she'd convinced herself she would see when he finally agreed to talk about the future, all she saw was the stricken look that crossed his face as the tickle came again.

He jerked his hand away, as if her stomach were radioactive.

'Zane? What's wrong?'

'I shouldn't have taken you like that. It was wrong of me,' he said, his voice so flat and dull and devoid of emotion her whole body chilled in the warm room.

'Don't be ridiculous,' she murmured, but she could feel the emotion closing her throat. 'Dr Ahmed told me conjugal relations are perfectly okay. We can make love right up to the third trimester, as long as we both want to—no harm will come to the baby.'

His eyes met hers, his expression so bleak, her throat closed completely. 'But that's just it,' he said. 'We're not making love, are we?'

Shock came first, quickly followed by pain and the brutal realisation that he meant it. And before she could think better of it, she said what she'd been wanting to say for months now, since before their wedding.

'I am.'

His gaze became hooded, wary. 'I told you I can't offer you that,' he said, as if he were reciting a treatise to a foreign power. Instead of addressing the woman he'd just made violent love to, the woman who carried his child.

'What about our baby, Zane? Can you offer the baby your love?' She could hear the edge in her voice. The anger she'd never allowed herself to feel for herself but which she suddenly felt for her child.

He thrust his fingers through his hair. 'We're both tired, and you need to get some rest. Let's talk about this tomorrow.'

'No, I want to talk about it now.'

The dark frown would have warned her off before. But he'd just destroyed this magical moment with his indifference—and if nothing else he owed her an explanation.

'Fine, Catherine. If you insist. No, I do not intend to love this child. I'm simply not capable of that type of emotion.'

She pressed a hand to her chest. Shocked by the flat tone.

'Why not?'

'You said it yourself—my own father was a monster.'

That's not an answer, she wanted to scream, but before she could get the words out past the boulder of stunned outrage in her throat, he continued talking.

'I think it best in the circumstances that we end our sexual relationship. I'll arrange to have your possessions moved back to the women's quarters. You're going to be busy between now and when the baby's born, finishing off your book. It's probably best if I don't distract you further.'

'Distract me?' she said. Horrified at the non-chalant tone. 'But I love you. I'm your wife, the mother of your child. I want us to be a family.'

'You don't love me. You don't know me. If you did, you'd know what you want isn't possible with a man like me.'

'Don't talk in riddles, Zane,' she snapped, the anger flowing freely through her now to disguise the crippling pain. 'What does that even mean? I can understand if you don't love me. I was will-ing to wait for intimacy and understanding be-tween us to grow. But you won't even try? And now you're telling me you won't even try to love our child either?'

She'd never raised her voice, never deliberately sought a confrontation. She'd blamed herself, her expectations, the circumstances, the timing.

Why had it taken her three months to see the blame for the empty spaces in their marriage lay with him? And his refusal to bend. Even in the slightest.

He was the one who had refused to talk about anything but the most superficial details of their relationship. He was the one who hadn't budged an inch since their marriage. He was the one who came to her every other night, as if he were on a schedule and then left.

She'd let him get away with far too much.

'You're tired and you're overwrought.' Gripping her elbow, he led her out of the bathing chamber and back towards her own suite.

She wanted to argue, to shout, to carry on, but the storm of emotions inside overwhelmed her. And the anger drained away until all that was left was the hurt.

She walked into the room, and he stopped at the threshold.

'We can talk more tomorrow,' he said. 'When you're willing to be practical.'

She collapsed on the bed as soon as he was gone. But then she felt it again, the flutter of their child. Wanting to be heard. Wanting to be loved.

Pushing herself up, she glanced around the ornate chamber. It wasn't his mother's room, but it was just the same, she realised. A gilded prison.

She had become trapped by her love for a man who could never love her back. The way her father had been trapped by his love for her mother. Trapped in an unhappy, insubstantial marriage.

Eventually Zane would stray. How could he not? He was a highly sexed man—he wasn't going to spend the rest of his life celibate.

She would have to watch him take lovers, the way her father had once been forced to watch her mother.

Their marriage would be an empty shell of duty and nothing more. A charade, to protect a child he couldn't even love.

Swiping the tears from her eyes, she sat up. She had to leave. What other option was open to her? She'd tried for three long months. She'd tried. But if she waited until the baby was born, she would be trapped here for ever. In this sham of a relationship.

Kasia would help her; she could make the journey tonight, through the desert to the Zafari border. Her heart bumped her throat, threatening to cut off her air supply.

She had to go, before she began to hate Zane.

He had been through so much, and had come out of it a strong, staggeringly sensual human being. But that wasn't enough.

Raising the sheet, she slipped out of the bed. And dressed quickly in the half-light, ignoring the soreness between her legs where he had taken her with such fury in the pool, and the wrenching pain in her chest at the thought of never seeing him, or this country, again.

You'll have his child. And that's enough. Even if it's a child he could never love.

However fascinated she was by Narabia's traditions, its customs and culture, and however invested she had become in its future—she owed a greater debt to her child. Their child. She knew what it felt like to be second best in a parent's life.

And if all of that wasn't reason enough to run, there was the biggest reason of all. Zane didn't love her. He'd made it very clear this was a constitutional arrangement—and tonight had proved his feelings weren't ever going to change.

Walking into the adjoining chamber, which she had been using as a study, she scribbled a short note—she owed him this much.

Hurt and sadness clogged her throat as she wrote, the tears she couldn't seem to contain slipping down her cheeks and splashing on the paper. She wiped them off. Then sealed the envelope and left it on the desk. He would find it tomorrow. By which time she would have had a twelve-hour head start.

She left everything behind her and secured the robe's veil over her face. If she was seen walking to the women's quarters with a suitcase, the guards would stop her.

As she left the room, she imagined Zane in the room next door. Arousal shimmered through her, combining with the empty weight in the pit of her stomach, which she doubted would ever go away.

'Goodbye, Zane,' she whispered.

Hopefully he would forgive her for leaving him. And one day, maybe she'd be able to forgive herself for falling in love with a Sheikh.

'Don't give me that crap, Kasia. I want to know where she's gone.'

Zane held onto the urge to shout at Catherine's friend. His mind reeling—the fury that had made his throat dry nothing compared to the stabbing pain in his heart ever since he'd found the note in her chamber. He'd gone in to talk to her, to try one more time to make her understand. But the paragraphs had pierced through the fog he'd been living in since leaving her in her room the night before.

I love you so much, Zane. I have ever since our night at the oasis. I should never have agreed to marry you without telling you. And I'm sorry for that. But I can't live with you knowing that you can never love me back.

If you change your mind about wanting to be more than a figurehead in our baby's life, all you have to do is ask and we can work out a custody arrangement.

But I can't stay in Narabia, knowing we are nothing more than a responsibility to you.

Please understand.

Love,

Cat xx

It shouldn't hurt this much. He knew that, but he couldn't think about that now. Because he couldn't seem to focus on anything except the driving need to find her and bring her back to the palace.

And Kasia was the key.

Catherine couldn't possibly have left without the girl's help. The palace guards would have stopped her.

'She told me nothing,' the girl said, her eyes defiant, but the tremble in her hands was a dead giveaway.

Kasia might be fiercely loyal to Catherine, but she was a terrible liar. He stepped closer and leaned into her face, his temper and panic impossible to contain any longer. He didn't want to frighten or bully the girl. But this was about Catherine, about her safety, and he was through messing around, because behind the panic lurked the fear—and it was starting to choke him.

'Tell me where she's gone, Kasia. Nothing will happen to you or her if you do, but if you don't, you could be putting her life in danger.'

'How?' the girl said, her whole body shaking now, the urgency of the situation finally having got through to her.

'She left alone, to drive across the desert in an all-terrain vehicle she doesn't know how to handle...' He had managed to discover as much from the garage manager, who had noticed the car missing that morning. But he had no idea which direction she'd taken. Had she headed to Zafari or in the opposite direction across the hills past the Kholadi Oasis towards Kallah? Either way it was at least a day's drive to the border, she had a ten-hour start on him and he only had one helicopter.

'But she said she could drive it,' Kasia blurted out, all attempts at subterfuge having fled.

'She can't. And there's no damn GPS signal in the desert—how would she know which way to go?'

'I gave her a map,' the girl admitted.

He fisted his fingers, resisting, barely, the urge to wring her neck. 'Which way?' he shouted, and the girl jumped.

'Zafari. She is headed to the Zafari border.' The girl's shoulders slumped, the defiance draining out of her.

'Get the motorbike,' he shouted to the coterie of servants and advisors who had accompanied him to the women's quarters. He would take it to the airfield, where the chopper was already fuelled and waiting.

As he walked away from Kasia the fury and panic and guilt were sucked into the gaping hole in the centre of his chest, until all that was left was the pain.

Cat squinted at the glow of red shimmering on the edge of the horizon. Her arms felt as if lead weights had been attached to her wrists as she wrestled to keep the Jeep on the road. Driving in the dark had been exhausting, as she'd tried to keep the unpaved dirt road through the rocky terrain between the glow of her headlamps, and mind-numbingly cold in the open-topped SUV. But she already wished for the chill again as the sun peeked over the dunes in the distance— painting myriad shades of red and orange across the sky, and bringing with it a wave of heat. She should have been at the border by now, but she'd had to keep the speedometer to below twenty miles an hour to negotiate the boulders in the rarely used road.

The vehicle's engine began to hum alarmingly, until she realised the metallic *swish-swish-swish* growing louder and more distinct wasn't coming from the Jeep. A shadow crossed over the bonnet and a huge black machine appeared overhead. She blinked, watching as it hovered in the air for several moments and then landed on the road thirty yards ahead, throwing up a cloud of sand and dust and blocking her path out of the country. Pebbles and rocks pinged off the Jeep's metalwork.

Cat braked, her dazed, exhausted mind struggling to take in what she was seeing. The silhouette of a man—tall and broad and looking far too magnificent in the traditional garb of black pants and tunic, boots and robe—jumped out of the chopper's cockpit and began walking towards her.

Zane.

She bent to rest her forehead on the steering wheel and dispel the foolish leap of joy in her heart.

When she lifted her head, he was almost upon her. She could see his face clearly in the dawn light. The pagan beauty of those sharp cheekbones, the sensual line of his lips now flattened in a tight line of displeasure or temper, it was hard to tell, the shocking blue of his eyes focused on her.

She felt as if she were floating—as the adrenaline that had kept her lucid for the last few hours drained away.

'Catherine, get out of the car,' he said, the deep commanding voice making her shudder.

Towering over her, he reached inside the Jeep to unlock the door. He pulled it open, then grasped her upper arm in firm fingers. 'Get out now. I'm taking you back to the palace,' he said, his tone low, as he tugged her out of the vehicle.

A last spurt of adrenaline charged through her, and she managed to yank her arm free of that firm grip. 'No, I can't go back.'

She wouldn't be able to leave him again. Wouldn't be able to find the strength. But then she swayed, her knees becoming liquid and he swore softly.

'You're exhausted,' he said, scooping her into his arms.

'Please, you have to let me go.' She thudded her fists on his chest, but the punches were weak and inconsequential and he didn't break stride as he carried her towards the aircraft.

At last he sat her down on the open cargo door. After ripping off her veil, he grasped her wrists and forced her leaden arms down to her side. 'Stop it, you're only going to hurt yourself. And the baby.'

The fear that had gripped her ever since she'd seen the helicopter became huge. 'I'm pregnant. I'm not an invalid.'

'But why would you put our child at risk?' he said, the veneer of indifference lifting to be replaced with something she'd heard in his voice once before—during their magical night at the Kholadi Oasis, when he'd told her about his mother. Not anger, but regret. 'Is it because you don't want it any more?'

'No, Zane, I want it very much,' she said. 'I already love it.'

The misery on his face became more pronounced. 'Then why did you run?' he said, his voice breaking.

And she knew she couldn't chicken out again. She had to tell him what she'd learned during the long night drive. What had made her more determined, not less, to leave him. 'Because what we have isn't a marriage, it's a business arrangement. And I don't want to live like that.'

He stiffened, his face grim. 'I made you my Queen. I've supported you in everything you wanted to do.'

'But you won't let me get close to you. You don't love me.'

'Why is that so important?' he shot back. 'I care about you. I want you—all the damn time. Why isn't that enough?'

She raised a shaking palm to his cheek; she felt the muscle bunch as she stroked the rough stubble. Despite everything, she wanted to soothe the sadness in his eyes. But the only words her dazed mind could generate were the truth.

'Because I won't settle for less than I deserve. The way my father did.'

He jerked his head back. 'What has this got to do with your parents? Is this some mad idea based on what happened when you were six?' he said, but he didn't sound accusatory, just devastated.

And suddenly she knew. She'd done the right thing. She'd believed that he was the only one who had to change, but the truth was, he wasn't. She'd let him get away with never examining his feelings for her—with giving her platitudes instead of promises—because she'd been scared. But she wasn't scared any more.

'What I'm saying, Zane, is that this is my fault as well as yours,' she said. 'My father was a good man, a kind man, but he was also a weak one. I always blamed my mother for the end of their marriage, because she left, because she couldn't remain faithful. But he was to blame too, for expecting so little from her. And I've been doing the same thing with you. I'm not going to do that any more.' She breathed deeply and gathered all the courage she'd gained in the last days, and weeks and months. Ever since climbing aboard Zane's plane and diving head first off a cliff.

'You made me your Queen. You made me your lover. But you refuse to make me your wife—in any real sense of the word. And I won't settle for less. I can't, or our child will be just like I was. And you were. Caught in the middle of a relationship that isn't real.'

The raw, aching wound inside Zane ripped open, the scar tissue no one but he could see tearing apart at her words. All he wanted to do was hold her, keep her safe. She looked shattered, exhausted, the bruised smudges under her eyes, the fragile shudders of her body, driving him wild. But she also looked so brave and indomitable.

The yearning he'd tried so hard to pretend wasn't there, that he'd convinced himself couldn't be true, welled up inside him like a tidal wave.

He tightened his grip on her arms, and dragged her to him, until his forehead touched hers, and her ragged breathing matched his own.

'Don't leave me,' he said in a shattered whisper, knowing he couldn't bear to ever let her go. That no matter what happened he would always want to keep her with him, and the child. To keep them safe and warm and his. 'I want you to be my wife. In every sense of the word, but I just...' He shuddered, the terrible fear consuming him. 'I'm not sure I'm capable of giving you what you want.'

Her cold hand caressed his face, and his heart shattered. 'Can you at least tell me why you think that?' she asked.

He would have to risk everything now, because he didn't just want her back, he wanted to know she would stay.

'Why can't we be a family, Zane?' she asked again. 'Why can't you love me—'

'Don't...' He slanted his lips across hers, feeding the hunger inside him he knew would never be satisfied. And silencing the words that cut him to the quick—words he knew he had brought about with his own cowardice.

All this time he'd been protecting himself. Determined not to see, not to acknowledge, what was right in front of his eyes: that he had fallen in love with her months ago. And this was the result. He could have lost her and his child.

She kissed him back, the sweet tentative licks of her tongue a benediction to his soul. He felt so tired all of a sudden, so weary of the lies, the subterfuge, the endless loneliness, the penance he'd forced himself to pay for so long.

At last he drew back and cradled her face in his hands, forcing her to meet his eyes. 'Catherine,' he said, tears he had tried so hard not to shed smarting in his eyes. 'I do love you. I love you so damn much I could hardly breathe when I found out you'd gone.'

'But…are you sure?' she asked, her sleepy hazel eyes so wide with stunned disbelief he almost wanted to laugh.

Until the amusement turned to shame.

He'd let her believe she was somehow unworthy of his love. When it had always…*always* been the other way around. He had never been worthy of hers. And now he had to tell her why. But first, he needed to come clean about his feelings.

'How could I not love you, Catherine?' he murmured, his voice hoarse with need. 'You're smart and courageous and compassionate and determined and so sweet…' He grasped her bottom and dragged her towards him until her thighs widened and her core was flush against the already prominent ridge in his pants. 'And every time you're in my arms, I know I can never have enough of you.'

The blush charged across her face. 'Then why

did you try so hard to keep me at a distance?' she asked and he knew his time was up.

'Because I didn't want you to know the man you'd married. It's all a goddamn facade, Catherine. The power, the sex, the invincibility.'

The small smile that curved her lips broke his heart. 'But I don't need you to be invincible, Zane. I just need you to be you.'

'You wouldn't want me if you knew me,' he said. 'If you knew what I did that night... I...'

She pressed her hands to his cheeks, forced his gaze to meet hers. 'Zane, whatever it is you have to tell me,' she said, the faith in her eyes only crucifying him more.

He tugged his head out of her hands, knowing he couldn't speak with her touching him, because then the truth would taint her too.

'That last night in LA after the argument with my mother, it wasn't a coincidence that my father arrived the next day.' Shame and disgust engulfed him. He struggled to breathe, to finally expel the words he'd never told another living soul. 'I contacted him. I called the Narabian embassy in New York.' The words choked up in his throat as the bitter guilt flooded back. 'I told them I was the Sheikh's son, that I wanted to be with my father. That my mother couldn't look after me any more. I knew she loved me, despite all the arguments, the money problems, the drinking…' He couldn't say the word, the disgust making his whole body shake now. 'But I begged them to contact him, to tell him. To take me away from her.'

A trembling finger touched his lips—and he was forced to look at her at last. 'Zane, don't… You don't have to say anything more.'

All he saw in her face was acceptance—and so the rest of it tumbled out.

'I didn't mean for her to die. She was an alcoholic. She was vulnerable and I deserted her when she needed me the most. After he told me she was gone, I knew it was my fault. That if I had stayed, if I hadn't been so selfish, if I'd managed to get away from him and back to her, I could have stopped her from taking the overdose. The only way I could stop myself from falling apart after she died was to stop myself from caring about anyone that deeply again. But my grand plan went to hell when I met you… Those feelings terrified me. They still do. It's why I can't even hold you after we make love, can't risk falling asleep with you and waking up with your arms around me. Why I'm scared to love the baby. What if I let you down the way I let her down? I never even said goodbye.'

'Zane.' Cat's heart shattered. He looked so tortured, the guilt and remorse making his broad shoulders slump, his beautiful face a mask of exhaustion. 'Alcoholism is a disease. She should have got help but she didn't. Don't you see that's not on you? It's on her. You were desperate and you were a child. You can't possibly be responsible for what happened after you left.'

'But even if that were true, I can't...' He jumped off the cargo bay, strode away from her, agitation in every step as he paced in front of her, thrusting shaking fingers through his hair. 'I feel as if I'm trapped by the events of that night. It never goes away, it's always there. What if it never does? How can I ever be a whole man if I can't get over what happened to me as a boy? How can I offer you what you need?' His gaze strayed to the soft mound of her belly. 'What our baby needs?'

She climbed down and went to him, taking his hands in hers, squeezing them tight. 'Stop it, Zane.'

He'd opened up to her, told her something she was sure he'd never told anyone else. He didn't understand yet how huge that was. But he would, because now, at last, they had trust. Something they could build on, which would allow them to share the pain.

He was scared. She understood that, because she'd been scared too. She'd been looking for intimacy, not realising that intimacy was the one thing he was most afraid of.

'We can make this work together, if you let me in,' she said. 'If you tell me how you're feeling. And if I do the same. If we communicate openly and honestly with each other we can overcome anything, even our fear.'

He pressed his forehead to hers and she heard the gulp of breath as he swallowed. 'Yes, yes, I want that. If it means I won't lose you, I'll do anything. If you can still love me knowing that I let her die alone...'

'Don't.' Cat flung tired arms around Zane's neck, her giddy heart racing as she buried her face against the strong column of his throat and inhaled that delicious scent of cedarwood soap and man and desert air—the love sweeping through her on a wave of emotion.

She kissed his chin and his cheeks, hooking her legs around his waist and letting him lift her into his arms. His deep sigh of relief reverberated against her chest as he sat down on the helicopter bay door with her on his lap.

'I love you so much, Zane. As long as you love me back, we can figure out the rest,' she said, pressing her cheek to his chest as she banded her arms around his broad body and listened to the strong solid beats of his heart. 'If you trust me.'

'I do,' he murmured, stroking her hair back from her face, then cupping her head. He lifted her mouth to his in a drugging, dizzying kiss, full of love and longing and hope.

As she watched the reddening dawn turn to gold on the horizon, she made herself a promise.

Whatever struggles lay ahead of them—as a new couple, new parents, a new monarchy—from this day forward they must never doubt their ability to overcome them, or the strength of their love for each other, ever again.

EPILOGUE

'YOU NEED TO stop that. She's supposed to be going to sleep,' Cat said, trying to sound stern, but it was next to impossible with the sound of her husband's deep chuckles and her daughter's high-pitched baby giggles echoing round their bedchamber—interspersed with the sound of loud raspberries as Zane bent his dark head to blow on his daughter's stomach and elicit a new round of laughter from them both.

As the game continued, the two of them totally oblivious to her admonitions, Cat found herself chuckling along with them, not sure whose enjoyment she found more wonderful, little Kaliah's or her father's. The brooding man she had first met a year ago in her old boss's office in Cambridge had almost completely disappeared now, she realised. He was still just as masculine and magnificent—and still far too overwhelming, especially in bed. But these days, he was so much more relaxed and approachable.

His daughter, for one, didn't seem to find him the least bit intimidating.

With her heart so swollen with happiness it was a wonder she could actually breathe, Cat lay back on the bed beside them, loving the sound of their joint laughter ringing off the bedchamber's luxurious Moorish furnishings, the intricately carved screens and mosaics. And wondered when exactly the change in Zane had happened.

Had it been during those first few months, when they'd been kidding themselves that they weren't in love while indulging in the insatiable sexual chemistry that continued to astound and excite her? Or later, after that heart-stopping declaration in the middle of the desert? Or had it been during the months after that, when he had finally been able to open himself up to the possibility of love after the traumas of his childhood? And had insisted on treating her as if she were the only woman in the history of the human race ever to have a child.

Well, you're the only woman who's ever had my child.

She grinned at the memory of his outraged exasperation every time she pushed back against his overprotectiveness—which was often.

Or maybe it had been after the birth of their daughter, when he'd held the tiny new life in his arms as if she was the most precious thing on earth—because, of course, she was—and declared that she had to be the brightest, strongest, most brilliant child who had ever lived, without an ounce of irony or hesitation.

Cat would have to agree with him there, because their daughter was as magnificent as her father, but then her gaze landed on the pile of toys Zane had insisted on purchasing for their three-month-old on their recent state visit to the UK.

Kaliah might be the brightest, strongest, most brilliant child who had ever lived, but Cat was going to have her work cut out preventing their daughter from becoming the most spoilt child who had ever lived too, when her daddy was so utterly besotted with her.

'Okay, Princess Perfect, you really have to go to bed now. I have some very important business to discuss with your mommy.'

'Good luck with that,' Cat murmured, her smile widening as she watched Zane finish buttoning up his daughter's sleep suit, then stand

and lift the little girl—who was still chortling and kicking—onto his broad shoulder.

'Do you doubt my ability to get my own daughter to obey me, woman?' Zane raised an amused eyebrow as he stroked his daughter's back, attempting to calm the baby down after all the activity—without a lot of success.

'Absolutely,' she said.

'We'll just see about that,' he replied. The sensual look he gave was one she recognised—but one she now knew hid a wealth of compassion and tenderness. 'I'm the Sheikh. My women obey my every command.'

'If you say so, Your Divine Majesty,' Cat said with a mocking smile.

'I'll be back in a few minutes,' he announced, busy rocking their daughter—who was starting to protest in earnest now at the prospect of actually having to do what her father told her for once. 'And when I return I expect you to be waiting for me. Naked.' His eyes darkened. 'So we can have that very important discussion,' he finished, then sent her a provocative wink before striding out of their room.

The room they had shared ever since her aborted attempt to run away from him.

A delicious heat rushed through Cat's body as she flopped back on the bed, still smiling—rather smugly now. It was going to take him longer than a few minutes to settle Kaliah, because their daughter was as headstrong as her father. But by the time Zane came back, she would be more than ready for that very important discussion.

As she waited, listening to Zane patiently attempting to soothe his fretful daughter to sleep in the room next to theirs, she decided it really didn't matter when Sheikh Zane Ali Nawari Khan had changed from the moody, intimidating man she had first met into a playful, protective and devoted father and the gorgeous, supportive and equally devoted husband and lover she adored so much today. Because all that really mattered was that he belonged to her and Kaliah and all the other children she hoped they would have together some day.

And that they belonged to him.

* * * * *

LET'S TALK

Romance

For exclusive extracts, competitions
and special offers, find us online:

- **f** facebook.com/millsandboon
- **⊙** @millsandboonuk
- **𝕏** @millsandboon

Or get in touch on 0844 844 1351*

For all the latest titles coming soon,
visit millsandboon.co.uk/nextmonth

Want even more
ROMANCE?

Join our bookclub today!

'Mills & Boon books, the perfect way to escape for an hour or so.'

Miss W. Dyer

'Excellent service, promptly delivered and very good subscription choices.'

Miss A. Pearson

'You get fantastic special offers and the chance to get books before they hit the shops'

Mrs V. Hall

**Visit millsandbook.co.uk/Bookclub
and save on brand new books.**

MILLS & BOON